CABIN ON THE SECOND RIDGE

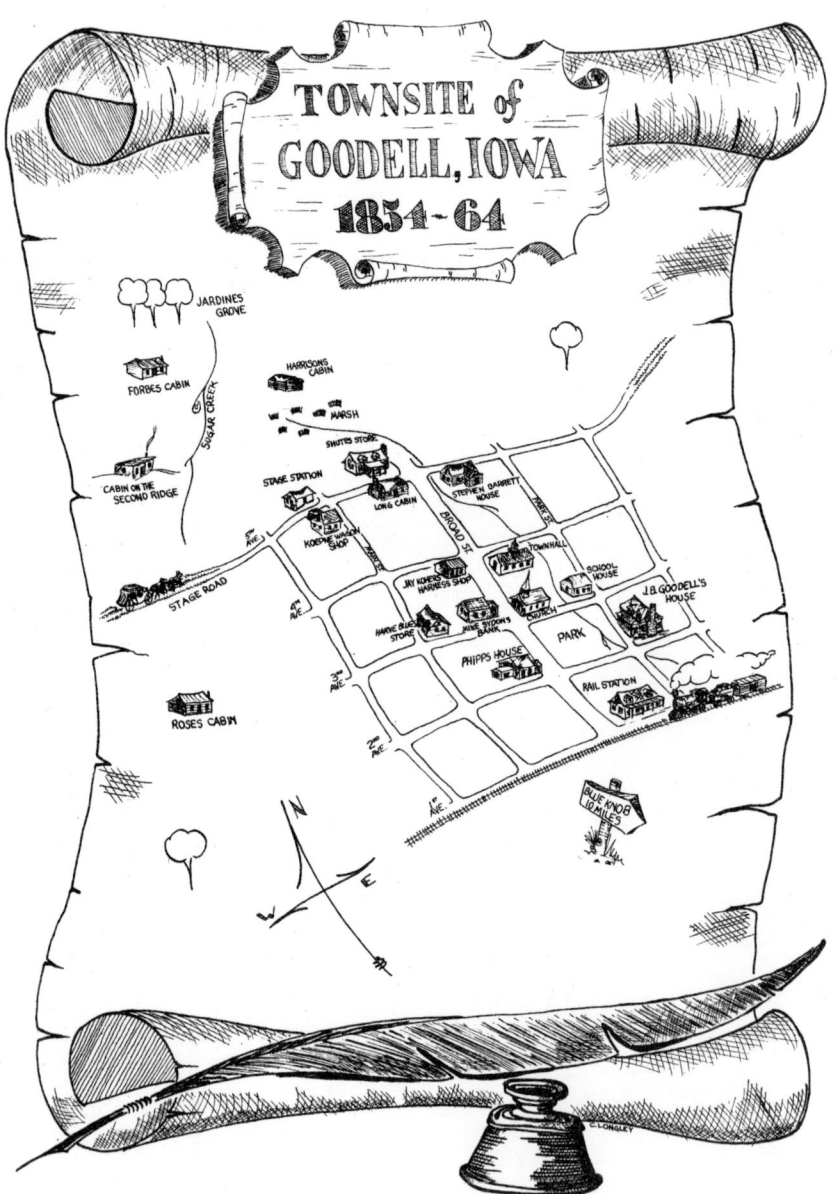

CABIN ON THE SECOND RIDGE

BY
RALPH L. LONGLEY

Illustrated by Charles Edward Longley

VANTAGE PRESS
New York / Washington / Atlanta / Hollywood

FIRST EDITION

All rights reserved, including the right of reproduction in whole or part in any form.

Copyright © 1976 by Ralph L. Longley

Published by Vantage Press, Inc.
516 West 34th St., New York, New York 10001

Manufactured in the United States of America

Standard Book Number 533-01969-9

To my sister,
Ethel Cordelia Longley,
who so carefully preserved
our family history.

CABIN ON THE SECOND RIDGE

Chapter 1

The bearded young man paced restlessly back and forth along the rough stone-paved steamboat landing, pausing often to look hopefully upstream. The wide expanse of the river held at the moment not even a raft of logs. Every few minutes he cupped hand to ear to catch the faint sounds of the engines of the St. Louis packet.

Emery Barrett's cowhide boots clattered noisily on the levee stones. In the town behind him the Saturday night crowds were beginning their noisy revelry, in the row of saloons that elbowed for position facing the river.

It was nearly dark, and a thin mist was rising from the river when the first faint throbbing of the packet's exhaust told of her approach. In a few minutes her running lights appeared rounding the wooded island and her oil-fed searchlight began stabbing into the dark, feeling for the channel, then swept the shore, picking out the landing.

At once a crowd began to gather. Travelers laden with their own luggage pushed their way through the curious townspeople. Roustabouts, blacks and white, appeared from nowhere, shoving and bantering among themselves.

As the packet swung closer to shore, Emery Barrett scanned the faces at the forward rail for his family. Yes — they were there at last. All his doubts and fears vanished.

Their shouted greeting was drowned by the clangor of the engine room bells and the mate's sharp commands as the steamboat was warped into the landing and made fast. As the gangplank touched the levee, Emery pushed his way through the crowd and rushed on board. There was time for only brief greeting, a hearty handshake from his father and a quick hug from his mother. Then, with Emery in the lead, they hurried ashore.

Halfway up the levee slope Stephen Barrett called a halt. "Set the baggage down here, and let's get our bearings. What accommodations do you have for us, son?"

"I've got two rooms for us right up here across from the landing at the Oglivie House. I paid for them and got the keys in my pocket. The place is so crowded. Mother and the girls will have to sleep three in a bed — you and Stan and I are across the hall."

"I'll just die if I have to go through another night wedged between mother and Ann," Philo, his youngest sister, complained in a shrill voice.

"I was lucky to get any rooms at all," Emery continued, paying no attention, "Settlers going west by the thousands. Looks like '55 will be a bigger rush for land than last year even."

There was pride in his tone.

"I hope you engaged the rooms till Monday," Stephen said quickly.

Emery smiled broadly. "I remembered you wouldn't travel on the Sabbath. I've never been in Muscatine on the end of the week. We'll see what it is like. It's a river town, you know."

"Now, mother," Stephen said solicitously, "you set the pace and we'll follow. You and Ann go ahead with Emery while Stan and Little Sis and I bring up the rear."

"Father, will you please not call me that again. Remember I am sixteen now," Philo spoke sharply.

Emery winked knowingly at his father. Philo hadn't changed.

Safely established on the second floor of the Oglivie House, Stephen and his sons rejoined the womenfolk in their room facing the landing. As they entered, Ann turned from the window and hurried toward her brother, put her arms around him and stretched to plant a kiss on his cheek. Holding him at arm's length, she said gaily, "Now I can get a good look at you, I do believe you've grown — and I like your whiskers trimmed pointed. You look well fed. Been learning to cook?"

"No, not at all," he replied, smiling down at her, "I've been boarding at Sarah Phipps's. You and mother will love her, she is such a good old soul. She insisted you folks come right there when you get to the colony."

"What about the house you are building for us?" Stephen asked anxiously.

"That is worrying me. I didn't get it near done. You see I had to haul most of the lumber from the mills here in Muscatine, and it takes seven or eight days to make a trip. It's quite a bit over a hundred miles from here to the colony."

"Where is your team and wagon?" Stanley asked.

"They're tied up in a feed yard over on Second Street. I always drive four on these long hauls, Bub. A man has to haul a real load to make it pay."

"I'm going to ride on the wagon with you and learn to drive four."

Philo, roaming the small room, poked dubiously at the mattress on which her mother lay resting.

"Just a bed sack filled with straw again! Oh, my aching back! And three in a bed!"

Ann turned on her: "Do be quiet! If your poor mother can stand it, you sure can."

The girl continued her investigating. "What is this funny sign doing here? It says 'Guests will please remove boots.'"

"Well, sis," Emery grinned, "out west here a man doesn't always carry along his night shirt and carpet slippers, so he doesn't always shed his clothes — or his boots."

"Pooh, that is nothing. Ann makes me wear my petticoat at night because it's got father's gold sewed into it. I'm loaded!"

"Hush, child, somebody will hear you!"

"I'm getting stoop-shouldered from carrying so much, and besides, it would be exciting to get robbed and maybe held for ransom."

"As I was saying," Emery went on calmly, "the proprietor puts up the sign to keep boots off the beds at least."

Ann laughed lightly. "Now when I get a husband — I'll teach him to take his boots off at the kitchen door."

"How are you coming along about finding one, Ann?"

"I've given up long ago, and I'm going to stay home and look after father and mother. Philo gets all the beaux that come our way."

"Yes and you should have seen the last one! The one that went to sea. He was so young he only had fuzz on his chin," Stanley teased.

"But Emery," his mother said very seriously, "you just said that people sleep in all their clothes! I hope you never did."

He grinned sheepishly. "I'd rather not say. It all depends on where you are and who you are sleeping with."

Emery continued quickly, trying to hide his embarrassment, "You folks will see some strange sleeping arrangements out in this country. Why, last fall when it first turned cold Anor Shute let Ben Howe and another fellow and me sleep in the loft over the general store with him and his wife and the hired girl."

"That sounds interesting," his father observed.

"Stephen Barrett! Remember you are a deacon in the church."

His eyes twinkled as he said, "That was last week, mother. I resigned before we left New Hampshire."

They had been talking for some time when Stephen rose and, taking his watch from his vest pocket, wound it as he stood at the window that opened onto Front Street. Ann laughed. "If father doesn't have our old clock to wind to tell us it is bedtime, he winds his watch. Do you see any sign of the town going to sleep, too. The noise doesn't sound like it."

"This is a river town, Sis."

Stephen continued winding.

"What about going to meeting tomorrow, folks? We should all thank the Lord for our safe journey."

"I hear that Reverend Robbins at First Church preaches very well. We might go there tomorrow, if you want to hear a strong plea for abolition. They call his church the "Uncle Tom's Cabin meeting house," Emery said, laughing.

"Oh, it's named after that awful book we all read a couple of years ago," Ann said earnestly.

"I had never stopped to think, son, but I suppose out west here slavery must be a pretty hot question."

"Gee, there was a runaway slave on the steamboat coming down river from Rock Island—and he was chained to a stanchion. I wanted to go talk to him, but father wouldn't let me," Stan said disappointedly.

"Yes, Emery, we all saw the poor fellow brought on board at Davenport. I talked to the man taking him back South, and you know he appeared a civil-spoken and businesslike fellow. I asked what he'd do with the Negro once he got him home, figuring he'd say, 'whip the tar out of him,' but all he said was that he'd put him to work again. Said he had been following the Negro all over east Iowa, always one jump too late because the slave was being hidden by the innocent-seeming Quakers, and passed along toward Canada."

"And the Yankee settlers like us at Goodell's colony do that, too," Emery said slyly.

Stephen shook his head sternly. "We will all go to hear this Reverend Robbins tomorrow, but we will have nothing to do with this 'underground railway,' as they call it. It is nine o'clock and time we were all in bed."

"Gee, but it would be fun to help slaves escape—like a real big game of hide-and-seek," Stan said.

Long after they had retired to the room across the hall, their voices droned on, with Stephen's earnest questions and Emery's answers. The younger man, full of enthusiasm for this new country, began to feel that his aging father shared his optimism. The doubts he had felt, concerning the whole family moving west on his recommendation, were fast disappearing.

Chapter 2

Stephen and Emery rose early on Monday morning, anxious to be on the road while the weather held good. As they started downstairs, boots in hand, Ann slipped quietly from the chamber across the hall.

"Glad you are up, my dear. We will need your advice about the furniture. Emery wants to get his freight loaded and be on the way. We three should eat right away—likely the stores aren't open yet."

Ann laughed. "I doubt if they ever closed. I wrote in my diary that there was more business done here on the Sabbath than was ever done in Bath, New Hampshire, on a weekday!"

As they stood for a moment on the plank walk in front of the Oglivie House, a Conestoga wagon, drawn by a jaded yoke of oxen, came up Front Street from the ferry landing. On its once white canvas cover it bore in crude letters the slogan 'Nebrasky or Bust.' A plow hung tightly lashed beneath the axle, and from its sides a motley array of pots and skillets swung, jingling with each jolt of the heavy wagon. A cow trotted nervously behind, her soft eyes intent on a very young calf bleating plaintively in the feeding box at the back.

"That man is getting an early start," Stephen observed.

"The ferry runs all night, father, when the rush is on. Their outfit looks new, like they were just starting out for themselves. Probably new married people. The oxen look fagged out like they'd come a long ways. They'll have plenty of company going to Nebraska, even if it is mostly Indian country yet. They say that one in ten that cross this river are bound there."

"I noticed his rifle was fastened to the wagon bows, handy," Stephen said grimly.

"He may need it."

Emery, striding ahead, paused at the sight of a man hurrying along on the other side of the street.

"Hey there, Ben. When did you get to town?"

The man hurried toward them with the quick step of a young fellow, yet his long straggling black beard and a shock of hair that curled up from the collar of his flannel shirt made him appear much older. Black-beady eyes, set close together beneath shaggy eyebrows, seemed piercing as he fixed his gaze first on Ann and later on her father.

Dingy wool breeches tucked into cowhide boots run over at the heel gave him an awkward gait. His hairy arms extended below the frayed sleeves of a checked shirt, over which he wore the remnants of a fancy vest. He removed his flat crowned felt hat at once and held it behind his back.

"Didn't know you were here either," he said in a flat nasal tone, without warmth.

"Yes, I came to meet the folks here. This is my father and my sister Ann, Mr. Howe. Ben is one of my best friends at the colony."

Ignoring Stephen's outstretched hand, he turned to Ann.

"I'm pleased to make your acquaintance, ma'am. Emery praised you till I felt like I know all about you."

Ann offered her hand hesitantly. He grasped it firmly and held it until Emery asked, "How come you are here at the river, Ben?"

"I'm driving Lol Phipps's wagon and four horses. Made it in a little over two days coming from Goodell with the wagon empty. I tell you it seemed like flying, Mr. Barrett, because I just own oxen myself."

"What are you hauling for Lol this time, Ben?"

"Oh, another plow for one thing, but mostly lumber. He is going to put partitions in his house and add a room. I sure wish the lumber was for me and my wife. You see I am a poor man, ma'am," he said, turning to Ann, "and when I bought the eighty acres, a sod cabin with a dirt floor was all I could afford."

His deep set eyes clouded momentarily. "We lived in it last winter, but it was bad for the boy—and her, too, poorly like she is, with the shanty damp when it rains and the floor always cold."

"How old is your little boy, Mr. Howe?" Ann asked with quick concern.

"Little Charley will be four this summer sometime, thank you, ma'am," he replied, looking down at her sharply.

"When did you get to town, Ben?" Emery asked.

"Late Saturday night. I could have got my load yesterday, but of course I wouldn't travel on the Sabbath."

Finally Howe could endure the delay no longer.

"I hope you folks will pardon me, but I've got to go to the store and then see to my load. I'm anxious to get started home. I've got sod corn to plant—and alone, too. Emery can tell you what a job that is. I'd figured on Laura dropping the seed while I cut the slits in the sod, but she's barely able to do the stable chores. I'll see you folks at the colony, soon, I hope."

With that he turned and crossed the street clapping the battered hat over his shock of hair as he went.

"Your friend seems in an awful hurry, son. Probably he is worried about his wife."

Emery chuckled. "More'n likely he is worried whether she is tending the stock like he told her. He is an odd character. I liked him at first, but that was before Laura came west. He turned out to be what folks call a one-gallused settler—hard up all the time and complaining."

"Poor man, he must have been glad to see his wife and their little boy again," Ann said sympathetically.

"No, he never acted like he cared about Laura. Imagine his

thinking she could drop seed corn for him this spring! Why, the last time I saw her she could barely hobble up the steps into Shute's store."

Ann looked up admiringly at her brother as she said, "I'm glad you don't let yourself get so bedraggled and down-at-the-heel-looking as that Mr. Howe. Do other men at the colony go around with such a mop of hair and scraggly whiskers?"

"No. And if Ben lived in the 'long cabin,' as we call it, the boys would hold him down and trim his hair and whiskers with sheep shears!"

"How come Mr. Howe escaped the shearing?" she said and laughed.

"Well, he doesn't live in the long cabin. He and his wife live way out on the second ridge west of the colony."

"I'd think his wife would have trimmed him up before he left."

"Likely she did suggest it, but knowing Ben, that would make him dead set against being spruced up—he is that bull-headed."

"Boo, I wouldn't like to have a husband that stubborn."

Stephen's eyes twinkled.

"Let that be a lesson to you, young lady. This man has already fooled one woman into marrying him."

They entered a small restaurant where the slovenly waitress welcomed Emery as a long lost friend.

"You must be a regular customer of hers, son."

"Well, I'm down here at the river about once a month, and I eat here each trip," Emery explained cautiously.

"That's all right, brother—we won't tell your Hannah Stover about the girl in Muscatine."

"By the way," Stephen continued jovially, "we saw Hannah just before we left home. Funny thing—she just said, 'I'll be seeing you folks.' That sounded like she might come west. You planning to get married?"

"Well, maybe, after corn picking."

"Fine, son, fine."

"I figure a man has a chance to make a good living farming this prairie land. I can take care of her here lots better than in New Hampshire."

Later, as the men talked, Ann sat silently looking out of the window.

It was midmorning when Stephen opened the door of his wife's room at the Oglivie House. Doshia and Ann sat knitting, while Philo leaned disconsolately against the frame of the open window.

"Well, mother, the wagon is loaded, furniture, lumber, doors and windows for the new house, and even the big boxes we shipped from home weeks ago. Our boys are already on the road. You couldn't have hired Stan to ride with us. He wanted to drive the four horses right away, but Emery made him wait till they got out of town."

Doshia rose stiffly from her chair and faced him accusingly.

"You mean that boy has started overland without anything but what he has on his back? Stephen Barrett! What were you thinking about?"

"Well, mother, the boys won't be needing nightshirts where they'll be sleeping. Fact is," he added, "we don't know where we will be tonight. The livery stable man where I hired our hack says we could make Iowa City by bedtime, if we get started right away—it's about forty miles."

"Then we aren't going in a stagecoach?" Philo asked plantively. "Who wants to be forever on the road in a buggy when we could get there quicker by stage?"

She turned toward the window petulantly and stood looking down the street.

"This must be the rig you hired coming now—looks like a chicken coop on wheels."

"I have hired a hack with a good driver," Stephen said with dignity. "It will be much better for mother than going by stage. We can stop over—"

"And make it last that much longer!"

"We'll go right down, soon as I get the boy to help carry."

Stephen, striding on ahead, paused at the sight of the vehicle waiting in front. The driver, a beardless boy scarcely older than Stan, sat holding a tight rein on a pair of lank, wild-eyed horses that stood pawing the ground. The boy never took his eyes from the team, even as Stephen said, "There must be some mistake. I hired a quiet team for this trip. My women folk, you know—"

"This is your rig, mister—from Duffy's stable. My old man used to drive for Frink and Walker afore they sold to Western Stages."

"But what about you, my boy? Have you driven this team?" Stephen asked skeptically.

The boy shook his head and gulped.

"They've hardly been hitched before—we had a terrific time—"

"What about another team?"

"Ain't any more—all hired out a'ready."

"Do you know the road beyond Iowa City?"

"Never been past the city. It's just a trail anybody can follow."

At sight of the women folks, the team shied away and threatened to overturn the hack.

Stephen set down the luggage heavily and, turning to Doshia who had seen the fracas, said as he grinned sheepishly, "And I spent half an hour talking that man Duffy into taking thirty dollars' hire for the rig' with a good driver and a safe team,' and I get this!"

"You must be slipping, father."

Stephen continued, "The boy seems to handle them well enough—here, anyway. There is no other way, mother. Trust in the Lord for a safe journey, and He will carry you through."

Reluctantly, the three women entered the hack while Stephen helped stow away the baggage. As he entered and closed the narrow door behind him, the team jumped forward, and the hack, lurching wildly on its leather thoroughbraces, moved rapidly down the rutted street.

Stephen braced his feet instinctively and took a firm grip on the frame of the door. The vehicle was gaining speed rapidly. From within it was impossible to see either the team or the driver. But, judging from the swaying and lurching, Bob, the driver, was fighting to control the team. People paused open mouthed as the hack passed.

Ann seated opposite appeared calm, almost amused as she reached for her mother's hand and held it. Her knitting bag slid to the floor.

Philo shrilled: "I don't see anything funny about all of us going to be killed!"

The hack lurched again, worse than before, and Stephen braced himself. He was trying to hide his own fears. The grim, set look on his face brightened momentarily as he looked up and said, "Philo was worrying about this hack being so slow, but at this rate we'll beat Western Stages."

The team continued their breakneck pace despite the moist warmth of the day. Flecks of foam tossed from their bits floated past the carriage. Their panting could be heard even above the rattling of the vehicle, and the pace did not slacken until the road began the long climb through the bluffs that edged the great valley. It was a long hard pull, and by the time the top was reached they had slowed to a trot. Stephen called a halt.

Standing beside the hack, he was silent for a full minute, with eyes closed, his right hand thrust deep into his coat pocket clasping the well-worn Testament he always carried there. Then for a brief moment his gaze took in the panorama that lay behind. Rising smoke indicated the town they had left—hours ago, it seemed. He took a long look as of farewell to all that lay to the East, the old life, the familiar things very likely he'd never see again. Resolutely he faced about, and entering the hack with a nod of assurance to the boy, said cheerily, "Let's be on our way."

The Barretts had ridden in silence for some time, and had passed numerous freight wagons, when Ann asked suddenly, "What became of our boys? Surely they didn't have this much head start."

Stephen grinned. "I caught sight of them as we passed back there when the team was running."

"Mother would have tossed Stan his long-tailed nightshirt to use on the road, if she had known."

Doshia Barrett could see nothing funny in the situation. She was riding with her eyes closed.

"We may not make Iowa City today," Stephen remarked. "We might have to sleep on the floor in some cabin tonight—and with all our daytime clothes on. We might as well start roughing it one time as another."

"I suppose we will pile up three in a bed again—if we get a bed," Philo complained. "And I'll have to wear my precious gold-filled petticoat both day and night."

"You may do worse than that," Ann consoled.

"Why did I ever come west anyway?"

"Adventure—romance—new faces—" Ann chanted.

"Huh!"

Fifteen miles from Muscatine the road descended a short hill into Cedar River Valley. It was a considerable stream, spanned by a narrow bridge without a railing. Cautiously the team set foot on the planking, then stopped short. Stephen reached for the door latch but the hack lurched ahead and he settled back trying to appear calm. The rawhide whined as it fell on the rumps of the team. The horses shot ahead, pushing and shoving at every step, trying to gain the center of the narrow bridge.

Once Stephen leaned toward the window as though hoping for some escape, but drew back at sight of the river, dark and swift, a few feet below. Above the rumble and creaking of the vehicle, Stephen's voice was scarcely audible as he said, "We will be across in a minute, mother be calm like I am."

Then, as suddenly as it began, the thunder of the horses' hooves ceased, and the swaying hack righted itself. The wheels touched dirt.

As the boy pulled the team to a halt, Stephen reached for the latch and got out. He leaned over and recovered his hat from the floor and carefully brushed it off. Within the hack, Ann was applying smelling salts to her mother.

As Stephen stood looking back, a covered wagon drawn by a yoke of oxen came onto the bridge and began ambling placidly across. As he turned to reenter the hack he remarked, "Give me a yoke of cattle every time—they have some sense."

Five miles beyond the river, the driver turned off the road at the midway stage station. The thirsty team inched forward toward the log watering trough, even as the Barretts were getting out. Still holding firmly to the reins, the boy called down rather plaintively to one of the stable hands to unrein them. The stable boss stood at the roadside shading his eyes against the lowering sun.

"He's looking for the stage that left the city at half after one," the driver told Stephen rather proudly, "and it will be in Muscatine before bedtime. And that is pretty fast for forty miles, I'd say, mister."

Philo came out of the tavern ahead of the others. She approached the hack and tried to strike up a conversation with their driver, but he paid her scant attention, for the team shied at sight of the girl's billowing skirts. She turned and reentered the hack before the others were ready.

With the passengers seated again, the tiring journey was resumed. Before long a blast of a horn announced the coming of the eastbound stagecoach. The hack veered sharply to the right as the stage flashed past, its gay paint blurred with mud and the dust of the road.

The boy leaned over and called to Stephen, "Did you notice how he hogged the road so I had to pull over! If this was a freighter he'd not 'ave done it."

It was nine o'clock when the hack stopped at the Hawkeye House in Iowa City.

Chapter 3

"Think we can make Goodell's colony by tomorrow night?" Stephen asked as he stood waiting impatiently beside the hack in front of the Hawkeye House the next morning.

The boy shook his head doubtfully. "It's a fur piece yet. The feed stable boss says it's eighty miles and the road gets worse. We have to ford the cricks."

"I wish my womenfolk would hurry," Stephen said uneasily.

"No use trying to hurry a woman," the boy observed sagely. "They might just as well enjoy this hotel while they can, because it'll be the last decent place they'll have to sleep."

"We have a regular house of our own at Goodell's colony," Stephen said sharply.

"I didn't mean no slight, sir. I was thinking where we'd likely be tonight. Me—I think I'll sleep in the hack."

"You mean there are no regular taverns at the stage stations?"

"Nothing but them stinking little cabins that takes in travelers, sir. That's what they told me at the feed stable. The way they laughed when they said we ought to make old man Burdine's by nightfall. I guess it ain't much of a place to stop."

"My women folks aren't expecting anything fancy, so I am sure they won't complain—except maybe my youngest daughter."

"Yes, sir, I know."

Beyond Iowa City the country was entirely different from that traversed the first day. For miles the stage road was only a narrow rutted trail through a heavy stand of timber. In the shaded dampness violets, bluebells, and Dutchman's breeches made a blanket of color. Emerging onto open prairie, blue flags poked their heads up through the tangle of old grass, as if to hide its drabness until the new growth.

The creaking and bouncing of the heavy loaded vehicle made talk difficult. Each of the Barretts appeared lost in his or her own thoughts. To Stephen each mile traveled meant one less to travel. He was anxious to see the farmland Emery had bought for them; and especially to see the new house in the settlement.

Doshia rode with eyes closed, wincing at every violent bounce of the hack. Each mile traveled took her father from "home." She felt certain she would never again see that comfortable white-painted farmhouse to which she had gone as a bride. The hard maples would be in leaf by now. Vaguely she wondered if Stephen and the boy driver could ever find Goodell's in this endless stretch of prairie where all the hills and valleys looked alike.

Philo sat looking glumly out of the window. Her father's talk of 'a nice house all ready for us' meant nothing to her. She would not be staying long anyway. Soon as I'm old enough I'll go back home and never come back to this God-forsaken country!

Ann Barrett glanced often at her mother's drawn face as though her own ready sympathy could ease the pain in her mother's old back injury. Reaching out a hand to clasp her mother's she was thinking, if we can just get to the colony and be settled so I can take care of her—and father.

Ann never thought very far ahead for herself. It wasn't necessary. Her father saw to it that his oldest daughter had all she seemed to want of the furbellows as well as the necessities. Each day, each week and year were happily filled with work done, either at home or for others in need.

The sun was still an hour high when Stephen leaned out to ask the driver, "How much farther to the cabin we talked about?"

"It can't be fur because they said Burdine's was only ten miles past the German colony, and we passed that most two hours ago."

"We will have to stop at the next cabin, whatever it is. My wife can't stand any more of this today!"

A little later the boy called down, "Here we are, mister, but it looks like we are late."

The hack stopped and Stephen got out stiffly. As he started toward the small log cabin he said with all the cheerfulness he could muster, "This must be a popular place."

Philo poked her head out of the door and taking one look at the cabin, groaned, "Three in a bed again. Tell me, once more, why did we ever leave home!"

No one paid any attention to her. Ann helped her mother down from the hack and stood supporting her. Stephen had gone to talk to the settler, a grizzled old man with a peg-leg, who continued to sit leaning against the cabin as he answered questions. Above the shouts of children playing in and out of the cabin, he could be heard saying, "You damn right you can sleep and eat here if you got the price. Always room for one more, I say. Go tell the old woman in there to stretch the beans and salt pok a mite more. Place to sleep and two meals—let's see—five of you'll cost you a five-dollar gold piece. No paper money, mister."

"But my wife," Stephen began, noticing the earlier arrivals, "she is suffering with her back, and she has to have a bed."

"They all say that, mister, but try routing me out of bunking with my old woman!"

"I'll pay extra if my wife and our girls can have a comfortable place to sleep—not on the floor, mind you."

"You're a Yankee—I can tell by your palaver, but you ain't tradin' me out of sleepin' in the only bed there is. We got shelf bunks in there, let 'em down from the wall of a night."

The old man spat and looked away as though it didn't matter whether the Barretts stayed or not.

Stephen, thinking to drive a better bargain, asked casually, "How long have you lived here, Mr. Burdine?"

"Five, six years. Why? You noticed my door already? Don't make no remarks about me using that blanket for a door—it's been doing me summer and winter."

Stephen turned and stood looking down the stage road to the west. After a full minute he turned to ask, "How far is Goodell's colony, Mr. Burdine?"

"Good God—you aimin' to take them ladies to that place— It's forty miles to the turn-off this side of Latmeier's tavern!"

"Yes, I know about the turnoff from my son's letters."

"Goodell's place isn't even on the stage road, Sets on the most God-forsaken ridge in the whole Nineteen Mile Prairie, as they call it."

"I know about the turnoff, and I know about Goodell's colony," Stephen said with some dignity.

"Then you know what you're gettin' into." The old man sighed as if to say, I've warned you.

"The boy sleeps in the hack," Stephen said. "Couldn't you shave that five dollars a mite?"

"Nope! Once I gets into bed it's all the same to me where any of you sleeps."

"I think we'll stay," Stephen said resignedly pulling out his purse.

As he hurried toward the women his face lighted. "We're all set," he said cheerily.

"You mean we are going to sleep in that—thing? And with all those people and children?" Philo said peevishly.

"Remember what Emery said about our seeing strange sleeping arrangements," her father said and chuckled.

When the tin dishes had been washed, Mrs. Burdine directed two men to set the table outside. After she lighted candles she went to pull the dirty blanket across the door. "There now," she spoke sharply, "we ain't going to have no peepin' from none of them men. They're all alike, old and young, I always say."

She cast an appraising look at Doshia, who sat wearily on a bench against the wall. "You 'n' your two git one of the shelf beds, account of your age. You other three women get the other bunk. That leaves me and my old man and the two kids for the bed."

Ann and Philo fumbled with the fasteners that kept the wide shelf against the wall. "Now look sharp when you lets it down," the landlady warned, "and kill any varmints that runs. You can pad up a bit with them blankets there in the corner—account of your ma being poorly."

Ann looked at the blankets and shook her head as she whispered to Philo, "We'd better not use them."

The three Barretts prepared to sleep in all their clothing but outer garments, which would serve as pillows. The other three women brought out nightgowns from their carpetbags and were standing in the middle of the floor wriggling out of their clothing when old man Burdine drew the blanket open. Poking his head inside, he asked slyly, "You women about ready in here?"

"What did I tell you?" his wife cackled.

Turning, the old man called to those outside, "Last one in pulls the blanket over the door!"

"But Mr. Burdine," Stephen protested, "with fifteen of us in here and one small window—"

"I don't aim to be waked up by some of you on the floor complainin' you're cold."

During the night Stephen Barrett slept fitfully stretched out on the bare puncheon floor or propped against the rough log wall. He had ample time to think of a lot of things. Sleepily he wondered if life at Goodell's was going to be anything like this. Shifting his position, he bumped into his neighbor. Never expected to sleep in a mess like this—at my age.

Hours later the birds in the timber nearby began making their sleepy sounds. From a distance and drawing closer came the strident cawing of crows. At once Stephen was back in the old farmhouse and the saucy crows lining across the sky were coming from the big tree in his hill pasture—time to be up and at the milking, when the crows come overhead. Strange how hard this featherbed is!

He awoke with a start when someone hooked back the blanket from the door, letting in the morning light. He arose stiffly and as he reached for his coat he glanced toward the bed against the wall. Ann raised her head and waved, smiling. "We will get home today, won't we, father?"

"Yes, daughter, someway," he declared grimly.

Chapter 4

Sarah Phipps put down her broom and went wearily to the door to look again for signs of the Baretts' arrival. From the crest of the big ridge where Lol Phipps had built their home near the center of Goodell's townsite, the Nineteen Mile Prairie lay as a vast panorama of rolling hills, treeless and turning slowly green. Under the warmth of the slanting afternoon sun, distances deceived. Miles to the south along the stage road, a white topped Conestoga wagon seemed adrift in an empty sea of billowing prairie hills.

At forty, Sarah Phipps was always tired. Mother of four, cook and housekeeper in a house scarce large enough for her own brood, she invariably greeted strangers seeking shelter with the quiet assurance that she would manage some way. To Sarah, taking in the Barretts till their house was ready was just her Christian duty.

She called to her children playing on a pile of lumber nearby, "Now you keep watching the trail for the wagon, or whatever it is. We don't know what they are driving. And Lol, I'm needin' more firewood presently."

Wild horses could not have dragged young Loyal, and June, a winsome miss of seven, from their lookout post. By some misunderstanding they believed that Emery's brother and one sister at least were young enough for playmates.

It was around four o'clock that little June let out a scream that frightened her mother, thinking it was another rattlesnake. Instead, she saw the children running toward the house yelling and pointing. A hack was coming up the ridge from the stage road.

"Lol Phipps, you come here this minute and get me that wood to poke up the fire for tea water."

"But mother, he's already gone!" June said breathlessly.

"Where'd he go so quick? Must a lit arunnin'."

"He went to ring the bell," June exclaimed.

A minute later, a bell began ringing wildly. At the window Sarah watched her fleet-footed son pulling on the rope. Suddenly a woman came barging out of the store nearby, shaking her fist at the boy. The ringing stopped.

"Sister Shute don't need to be so touchy. The idea—stopping the bell when new folks come to town!"

Sarah took a quick look about, as if to see what more could be done to make appearances better. She made a quick flourish of the broom out of the door, tucked a few more odds and ends out of sight, and stuffed the last stick of wood in the cookstove, with the tea kettle pulled forward to heat better. Then she tied on a gingham apron and, smoothing down her hair, went to the door.

Stephen got out first and stepping briskly, came to meet her, saying, "I know you must be Mrs. Phipps from the way Emery spoke of you. We are so glad to be here—and safe," he added.

He turned toward the hack. Ann had hopped out and was helping Doshia step down. She seemed dizzy and with Ann on one side and Sarah Phipps on the other, moved slowly toward the house.

Meanwhile Philo got out on the other side and stood looking about. Scarcely a dozen low unpainted houses and a few covered wagons stood scattered at random over the quarter-section townsite. The houses, small and squat, seemed dwarfed against the bare background of empty paririe and cloud-blown sky. All were alike in at least two respects. They were perched on boulders—and from their unpainted walls stovepipes elbowed out and up. There were no chimneys.

Philo turned to pick up her own small portmanteau and with a show of great effort started slowly toward the house.

Sarah's son, Loyal, returning from his brief turn at the bell, stood watching the driver unload the luggage. After Stephen had left, he asked anxiously, "Are you Emery's little brother?"

"No, sonny, I'm the driver," He said and then added proudly, "clear from the river."

Young Lol was disappointed.

"Say, sonny, where does a man tie up his team for the night?" he asked patronizingly.

The boy pointed up the road. "There's a feed yard up there, mister, beyond the bell tower and the flagpole— you have to water in the slough back of Shute's store."

"I'll be going, then."

"Wasn't there a little boy—of his?" he said, pointing to Stephen.

"Wasn't any boy in our party— just the old gent and the three women."

The boys's face clouded.

"Where can I get a meal, sonny?"

"Ma feeds strangers, but we're full up now. Lydia Forbes takes boarders. That's her place up there, the one with the funny roof."

Meanwhile Doshia rested in Sarah's one rocking chair sipping tea and sampling freshly baked ginger cookies.

"My, I did feel so faint when we first stopped," she murmured. "I don't know what I'd do without Ann—she is so good to me—and then you folks taking us in and all."

Sarah Phipps assured her she would have it no other way.

"You just make yourselves right at home here. Your house isn't done yet. Emery has sure been trying to have it ready, but spring is such a busy time with farming to do."

Little June came and stood in the doorway, closely watching Philo who wandered about the crowded room, pausing only long enough at each window to glance out. At the front door the girl paused longer, to watch the hack being driven up the road.

Little June came and stood looking up into her face.

"Want to see my doll?"

After a long silence the child continued, "We're going to have school come fall and my brother and me are going. You going, too?"

"No, I've been."

"We have Sabbath school, and mother teaches us girls. You sure you don't want to see my doll? I made her out of corn husks."

Ann could not endure her sister's indifference.

"Can't you pay her a little attention? She wants to be friends because we are living here in Goodell from now on."

"Oh leave me be, can't you?"

With reviving strength, Doshia began looking around her. She apologized for crowding in upon the Phippes. "I'm sure Stephen will find our house is near enough complete for us to move right in," she insisted.

"Land sakes, there aren't any windows in it yet. I guess Emery has them on his wagon this trip."

"I can't help worrying about my boys—on the road that way. So much can happen."

"Now, Miz Barrett, I'd not worry about them. Of course we all worry about something. This very morning my husband says, 'Do you suppose Ben Howe will get back with our teams before bad weather sets in?'"

Ann brightened. "We met your man in Muscatine on Monday. I remember him. He looked so — well, different some way."

"Hadn't he left the river yet? He must have got there Saturday! But we might know he wouldn't turn a wheel on the Sabbath. He is so religious in a way. Ben is terrible slow about some things and fast about others — like gettin' his wife in the family way and her half-dead with consumption."

Ann was blushing as she said quickly, "He was in an awful hurry when we met him. He told us about his wife being poorly and about his little boy."

"Well, I must say Ben is dependable," Sarah continued somewhat grudgingly. "We trust him with money to pay for his load at the river."

A little later, Doshia and her daughters walked slowly the grass-grown road toward the center of the colony and the new house. From the open prairie beyond the townsite, half a dozen milk cows were being driven by three yelling, barefooted boys. Ann was thinking that it was just like back home — the sun going down, the smell of wood fires and supper cooking and the cows coming in from pasture.

Philo, walking alone, called back over her shoulder, "Did the old lady say this little shanty was their meetinghouse? No bell! No steeple! And not even painted!"

Ann and her mother walked on silently.

"So that's the 'long home' over there. Looks like a cow shed with a curved roof, to me. What a fuss Emery made over that!"

"But sister, they only had green lumber to build with. That cabin is home, to a lot of men till they can do better. Emery slept there for months."

"Oh."

Meanwhile, Stephen, who had preceded them up the path, stood at the door of the long cabin talking with a short, squat man of forty, bald except for a fringe of hair that curled back over the open collar of his faded shirt. Extending a hard, calloused hand, he greeted Stephen warmly.

"Mine is Forbes, Will Forbes, though some call me 'Deacon.' I was working out on my quarter section when I heard the old bell aringing and I says to myself, 'That will be the Barretts coming.'"

"Sarah Phipps says you have a houseful boarding and sleeping in this cabin of yours."

"That's right. The two in sight eat with us at first table."

"When do the others come in? It's near sundown already."

"Most of them are farming out on the prairie. They drive back nights—put their oxen in the feed yard and eat and sleep here. If a man fails to come in before dark, we run up a lantern on the flagpole so he can find the town. It's easy to get lost on the prairie."

"I see. It's like a lighthouse, isn't it?"

"You just as well meet these two, Mr. Barrett. Town is so small everybody knows everybody." Nodding toward the young man at the wash bench beside the cabin, he said, "Here you, come and meet Emery's father. This is Henry Laurie— practically one of the founders of the colony here—came along last spring in time to help stake out the townsite."

Henry Laurie put down the brush and comb and stepped forward briskly. He was a short stocky man of about thirty, whose round ruddy complexioned face broke readily into a smile.

"Welcome to Goodell, Mr. Barrett. We've been hearing a lot about you folks—from Emery—about the girls coming—and all. Well, I mean," he stammered and his face reddened, "I hope you folks trade at our store instead of sending to the river or to Iowa City."

"Henry works for Anor Shute in our general store next door," Forbes explained, indicating a small story-and-a-half building with a wooden awning extending over a platform that ran across the front. "He practically runs the business."

Young Laurie grinned. "I just came along looking for a job and liked the place, Mr. Barrett. I hope your wife and daughters like it here, too. If you'll excuse me, I've got to eat early so I can milk before time to tend store."

"And this is Bert Hillman," said Forbes, pointing to the tall, bashful-appearing young man of about twenty. "He eats at first table Wednesday nights. It's his night to go see his girl. Women are so scarce around here that a fellow can't afford to chance being late."

"It isn't the only night he goes to see her," Laurie called back from the doorway.

"Now, Deacon Forbes, I'm going over to see Will Harrison about a job on the house he is building out on the first ridge," Hillman stammered.

"That's all right," the deacon assured him, winking at Stephen, "Susan is a real nice girl, and we old fellows understand."

From inside the cabin, Lydia Forbes could be heard calling, 'Will, I thought you were in a hurry to eat, and there you stand amoonin'."

"Nice fellow, that Laurie. Has quite an eye for business."

"Well, Deacon Forbes, I'm keeping you from supper, and I see my women folk are coming to look at the new house."

As Stephen strode briskly across the tall grass, he was catching his first real glimpse of the bare unfinished house and thought, is this what we have come all this way to live in? With pretended cheerfulness he called out, "See here, mother, the street is going to be here," indicating a stake half-ridden in the grass, "must be laid out six rod wide. Pretty soon we'll be calling it Broad Street, and it will be all built up with fine houses like ours."

Doshia looked at him sharply, and wondered.

Ann, in the lead, stepped up into the bare shell of a house and sang out, "Oh, this is going to be real nice—two little bedrooms, a sitting room, and a kitchen— and we have a cookstove all ready to set up, but where's the chimney?"

"Stop worrying about that," her father said and laughed, "we'll run our stovepipe out a window like our neighbors do. We can get that sort of thing at Shute's general store. I was just talking to a young man name of Laurie who works there, and he—"

Philo brightened. "How old is he?"

"I'd say about thirty."

"Huh, Ann can have him," she said and sauntered to the doorway and stood looking across the prairie. The last rays of sunlight were touching the grassy slopes, turning them to a deeper green. Along the small stream that meandered through the nearby slough, red-winged blackbirds and meadowlarks sang their evening songs until a teamster brought his oxen to drink.

Chapter 5

Supper at the Phippses' was a pleasant meal, and the jovial Lol left no doubt that their hospitality was genuine. Still, there was no mistaking the fact the house, small and partitioned only with blankets hung on wires, was too crowded.

After supper, Stephen and Lol sat talking while Ann reset the table for the children.

"We're going to have a real university right here," Lol proclaimed proudly. "J. B. Goodell puts twenty-five dollars from the sale of each lot in the townsite into our building fund. I'm one of the trustees. We've got three thousand dollars in the Iowa City bank, and by the time all the lots are sold we'll have a tidy sum."

"I'm glad to hear about the university. Education and religion make a town amount to something," Stephen commented.

"We're getting the school started in the fall—I've hired Lon Bigsby's oldest girl to teach. And of course we've held meeting every Sabbath since the colony started. Church must have fifty or sixty members by now."

"Doshia and Ann and I plan on joining right away."

Soon after, Sarah suggested they all retire even if it was early, and the Barretts went gratefully to the beds assigned them.

After breakfast the following morning, Ann went with her father to the new house. Despite the cordiality of the Phippses, it was plain that the Barretts were overcrowding them. Anxious to be in his own house, Stephen decided to set up housekeeping with what essential bedding and utensils contained in two large wooden boxes shipped weeks before. Emery had freighted them from the river on a previous trip.

Wielding a broom, Ann set about clearing the rubble of building from the house. Stephen was busy uncrating the new cookstove when he called to her, "We will need stovepipe and some fine wire to tie it in place."

"Shall I go over to the store now?" she asked eagerly.

"You might as well—and get two pipe elbows. Mr. Shute or that young man will trust you for that little—I left my wallet with your mother. Tell him we will pay when we get our dry groceries this afternoon."

"Philo is getting awful tired of wearing that petticoat with all the family hoard in it," Ann said. "What are you going to do with the rest of the money?"

"It will go fast enough. Lol Phipps offered me forty acres for a hundred and twenty-five dollars. Land is going up, with talk of the Mississippi and Missouri Railroad coming through. Lol has this forty just east of the townsite and he says it lays right up to the railroad survey. I think I'll buy it, though not for the reason he suggested."

"Why did he want you to buy it?"

"He said it would make a good wedding present in case one of you girls got married," he said and "I told him we wouldn't be needing wedding presents for a long time, with Philo still so young—but I think I'll buy it anyway."

Despite protests from the Phipps, the Barretts moved their luggage late that same day. "But you don't have windows or doors yet, and it might turn cold and, besides, we are due for a rain. I'm hoping Ben Howe gets in with my outfit before it starts."

"You folks have been mighty kind, but we've got our hearts set on being in our own house before the boys get here with the freighter."

That night, long after the others had gone to sleep, Doshia Barrett, lying awake, heard the muffled creak and squeal of wagon wheels, and wakened Stephen.

"How do you know it's the boys?" he muttered sleepily. After listening, he agreed. "It's Emery! I never could teach him to stop and grease an axle when he was in a hurry." He lit the candle lantern and went out to help put the teams in the low stable behind the house.

Chapter 6

"I think it's just wonderful you taking that class of boys in Sabbath school," Lydia Forbes declared as she tossed the dish water out of the door of the long cabin.

Ann Barrett stood at the shelf wiping the last of the tin dishes. She turned to the older woman and said, "But Lydia, I have been hoping they'd ask me. Now I feel like I belong here in Goodell."

"Well you've got yourself a job is all I can say. My boy says you make Bible stories so interesting. Being as Will is a deacon it does seem as though our own boy should behave and pay attention. Rollin has always been so restless in Sabbath School—till you came. How do you manage to keep them quiet and learn them anything at the same time?"

"It seems easy— I'm used to boys—little ones."

"And there is such a difference in their ages—why that little shaver of Gerty Buderfa's is only about six, and his brother Bud must be twelve, because I know he is a year younger than my Rollin. But how do you keep them still?"

"Well you see I know boys—I practically raised my brothers after mother became so poorly."

"You are always busy helping other people, aren't you?"

"But I like to help people where I'm needed."

As she finished her work, Lydia sighed as she said, "It seems like I never get done with a meal until time to start settin' the table again."

"Most of the men go to bed pretty early, don't they? I've noticed the lights go out soon after Shutes' store closes."

"I don't know what the men of this town would do without Shutes general store for swapping yarns and passing the news," Lydia said.

"Yes, I know. Emery and Stan go over there every evening, and even father sometimes."

"Henry Laurie says that working there and listening is better than taking the Iowa City Paper because there is more town news and the rumors are fresher."

"Father heard Western Stages are going to come through the colony two days a week! Isn't that grand?"

"Then maybe we'll get a post office and the men won't have to go four miles to Latmeir's tavern to get the mail."

Ann laughed. "That will please Philo—she is always after the boys to go get the mail."

"Last Sabbath, after meeting I heard Julia Goodell and Amelia Hanlon talking about organizing a ladies' society to sew for the poor and help raise money for the new meetinghouse."

"Oh, that would be nice," Ann agreed. "Some of those poor people still living in covered wagons will need help come winter."

"Yes, and even some of our own church folks—like the Buderfas," Lydia hastened to add under her breath. "Poor Gerty has a hard time even with Jim working steady in Captain Clack's flour mill. The old miser doesn't pay wages."

Ann asked, "Where did the Buderfas come from?"

"Missouri! Likely they are the only ones in town not for abolition."

Ann said thoughtfully," I guess it all depends on what a body was brought up to think."

"Well, Amelia Hanlon may be all in favor of starting a sewing society, but she won't be going for quite a spell—her showing as much as she does even wearing that cape."

"I keep thinking about that poor Laura Howe. She must be about as far along. She hasn't been to a meeting since that first Sabbath after we came to town. She is so thin and—"

"Land sakes," Lydia interrupted, "Shute's closing up. Must be bedtime. I hear the men coming into the bunkroom."

As Ann hurried toward home, her two brothers, chuckling to themselves, caught up with her.

"What's so funny?"

"Oh, wait till we get in the house. Father will want to hear this."

As they entered, Stephen arose from his chair and, reaching for the Bible, said, "Bedtime—and now I'll read—"

"But father, we've got all kinds of news to tell."

Stephen put the Bible back on the light stand as he said, "Well, I guess the Lord can wait a bit."

"Stephen!"

"They were telling about J. B. Goodell buying a horse of a settler down Blue Knob way. It seems the woman and children came out crying and took on something terrible about selling their dear, beautiful horse and—"

Doshia was immediately sympathetic. "Poor woman, I remember how I felt when your father sold our Dolly for fifty dollars."

"Mr. Goodell was paying a hundred for this one, though."

"Whew! And you're meaning to tell me the horse wasn't sound!" Stephen exclaimed.

"Of course not! And she was balky, too. That was why the woman cried and acted up like she did—to hurry the Reverend Goodell into taking the nag thinking he had a bargain."

"It seems just awful for the settler to beat a minister in a horse trade," Doshia said earnestly.

"It's like I've always told you boys—anything is fair in a horse trade. What else did you boys hear tonight?"

"They say there won't be much of a celebration on the Fourth. Just a town picnic dinner at the schoolhouse. No parade, no reading of the Declaration, and not even a patriotic speech. Sam Cook the lawyer is too busy hoeing corn to figure out a speech this year."

Philo was indignant. "You mean all this town is going to have is a stuffy old picnic in that shanty? Well, I'm not going one step."

Ann spoke reassuringly, "Never mind Philo, Susan Harrison is planning a hayrack ride and picnic for the Fourth. There'll be at least a dozen girls all the way from little Minnie Buderfa up to Debbie Hart—you and I come in between there somewhere. Susan's brother is going to drive."

"I pity him, drivin' for that screeching mob," Stan said.

"Where are we going—down to the timber near Latmier's post office?"

"No, I think we are going to Jardine's timber—it's closer."

"I'd rather go to Latmeir's so we could get the mail. Stan won't go only once a week," she complained.

"She is still looking for a letter from that beau that went to sea before we left New Hampshire," Stan teased.

Stephen picked up the Bible again. "I will begin now."

Chapter 7

"I say it would have been better if Laura Howe's baby had been born dead," Gerty Buderfa declared firmly.

A murmur of disapproval ran among the ladies of First Church sewing circle gathered for the first fall meeting in Julia Goodell's new parlor.

"Likely it won't live long anyway, puny as they say it is—from Laura being so run down and all," Gerty continued, glancing around the circle as though defying contradiction. "If I do say so, it would be a blessing if it was taken soon. Laura ain't long for this world."

"Oh Gerty, you can't mean that," Ann Barrett said reprovingly.

"The Lord gives and the Lord takes away, I always say," Gerty continued. "It's Providence that takes a little mite when there's no one to take care of it."

"I don't think we should talk as though Laura was surely going to die," Sarah Phipps said tartly. "There's always hope. We know Doctor Tom will do all he can for both of them."

"It will be better if the baby is taken first. You women know as well as I do there ain't nothing quite so pitiful as a widower left with a baby to bring up."

"He could marry again," Miss Debbie Hart hastened to suggest. "Some woman to take care of the baby and make a home. And there's the four-year-old, too."

"No woman who knew anything about Ben Howe would ever marry him," Mrs. Bigsby said under her breath.

"You never can tell," Miss Debbie said with a knowing smile.

After a silence of several minutes, Julia Goodell looked up from her sewing and said, "I've been thinking if one of us could take Laura in and nurse her, perhaps she could get well."

"Not much chance of her gettin' well from consumption, babe or no babe!"

"Maybe it is my Christian duty to have her brought here," Julia Goodell interrupted Gerty's continued pessimism. "She could have this parlor — we hardly ever use it, and it is plastered, too."

"Now Julia, you've no call to wear yourself out nursing a settler's wife. If you ever do," Gerty warned, "you'll find yourself saddled with that boy to raise."

"But he is such a fine little fellow." Ann looked inquiringly across the room to her mother. "Surely some of us could take him."

Doshia Barrett avoided her daughter's glance.

"Laura should 'ave made old Ben sleep in the stable them nights last winter when he got ideas," Gerty cackled. "She'd have saved herself and other folks a lot of trouble!"

Philo snickered.

Lydia Forbes remarked how lucky the Goodells were in having their new house plastered. "Some folks seem to think that long cabin we live in is such a wonderful home, but believe me it's no place to live in cold weather. Will is trying to get old Simon Dennison to get our new house plastered so we can move in."

"I am not one to bear tales nor complain," Mrs. Bigsby said, making each word count, "but my Lucy says she is going to close school if the men of this town don't get the schoolhouse plastered right away. The idea of them building a fine two-room school and then never finishing it.

Late the next afternoon as Ann walked up the road from visiting Sarah Phipps she saw Ben Howe crossing the townsite half-walking, half-running. She watched him till he reached Dr. Holt's house. She did not mention the incident when she arrived home. A little later she appeared surprised when her mother called from the window, "There is Tom Holt going west on horseback, and I do believe it's Ben Howe riding double behind him."

"The baby must be worse," Ann said in a low tone.

"Yes, child, it does look that way."

"I thought it was just awful what Gerty said at sewing circle — about the baby being better off dead."

"Yes, it was a cruel thing to say with Mary Holt right there, and heartbroken over losing little Lucy only three weeks ago."

It was dusk when Tom Holt tied his saddle horse to the rail in front of Shute's store and made his way to the stove in the center of the crowded room.

"Is Ben's baby worse?" Henry Laurie asked quickly.

"How do you know where I've been?" Tom asked gruffly.

"Oh, here in the stores we get word of what goes on, even before it happens," Henry replied airily.

"Well, if you must know, the infant is in bad shape," the young doctor said dejectedly. "I wanted Ben to bring Laura and the baby to town for somebody to take care of—"

"And Ben wouldn't hear to it," Will Forbes finished the younger man's sentence for him.

"He acted like he didn't think Laura needed any help taking care of her own baby!"

Henry Laurie came from behind the counter and approached the stove. "I can tell you why he doesn't want them brought to town. He is independent. Hates to ask favors because he hates to do favors. Once he takes a notion in his head he is set in his way."

It was after midnight when Dr. Tom was aroused by hammering on his door and rushed across the townsite to deliver Amelia Hanlon of twins. And at about the same time, in the lonely sod cabin out on the ridge, Laura's baby died.

Ann Barrett heard both bits of news early the next morning, and from the same messenger. As she went about her morning work, she found herself wondering about Laura. Did she really want to bear this baby, knowing her own weakened condition? Perhaps it was Mr. Howe wanting another boy. She stopped, amazed at her own solicitude for these settlers she scarcely knew.

The evening after the Howe baby's burial, Ann and her mother were finishing the supper dishes when there was a knock on the door. When Doshia answered, Homer Hanlon stood waiting.

"Come right in, Homer. And do tell us about the twins. How is Amelia?"

"I'm in a great hurry, Mrs. Barrett, because I came to ask a favor. You see, all of this is a great surprise to us—the twins, I mean."

Doshia was smiling understandingly.

"Amelia keeps asking 'When is Ann coming?' So I came to see if you could spare her to help us a few days." He looked pleadingly from one to the other.

"What were they, Homer, both boys?"

"Land of Goshen, I've been so upset over the whole affair that I forgot what Jim Harrison's wife did say."

Ann suppressed a laugh to say, "Do they look alike?"

"You mean do they look like Amelia or me? No, and they don't look like anybody I know," he added, mystified.

"You want me to come over in the morning?" Ann asked.

"Oh, if you could, Miss Ann—and I'll gladly pay you—whatever you ask."

When he had gone, Philo came from the sitting room laughing. "Old Homer acts like he was surprised it was twins! Everybody else knew it—even father. Weeks ago I heard him say—"

"Child, the men folks might hear you!"

Next morning as Ann started across the townsite toward Hanlon's, Henry Laurie was at the well behind Shute's store. He waved to her, and as she approached he grinned broadly saying, "It's a small world, isn't it, Miss Ann? Here I am, pumping water just like I was the very first time I saw you walking up the road from the Phipps' to see your new house away last spring."

"How come you remember such a trifling thing as that, Henry?"

"I'll never forget it," he stammered, his face reddening, "because that was the minute I decided to stay in Goodell."

"How funny—your deciding that when you saw me."

"I thought things were going to come just right for me—after you came to town. But they haven't. Here I am still Anor's handy man, still pumping water as the same lovely maiden passes by."

"Now I am sure you're making fun of me for wearing this old work dress and with a shawl around my head."

"I think you look real nice. Today you wouldn't be wearing your best dress to go over to help the Hanlons."

"How did you know where I'm going, kind sir?"

"At the store we hear things before they happen. Why, I can even tell your future, young lady."

"Oh, I'd love to hear it sometime. By the way, I suppose you will be at singing school Friday evening."

"I'll sure be there if Anor will let me off. I like to go lots better since you came to town."

"That's a likely story! You always sit on the back row with the young fellows, and you never even notice who is there—and you walk home alone."

"But I'm bashful."

"You don't seem to be when I'm around. I've noticed how nice you sing when you are alone. I remember the first time I ever heard you—you were sitting right over there pailing Shute's cow and singing that new one we'd just heard, 'Sweet Sixteen.'"

Henry grinned sheepishly.

"I didn't know you were around."

"It sounded nice. I like your voice, Henry."

"Is that all you like about me?"

"I'm not going to answer any more of your questions, now."

"Will I see you at singing school Friday night?" he persisted.

Ann turned to go. "Yes, I want to come."

As she approached the farmhouse at the western edge of the townsite, Hanlon's cow stood peering through the rail fence bawling mournfully. Inside the stable a small calf blatted hungrily.

The young minister came bustling to the door, embarrassed that she had arrived before he had straightened up the house. Ann smiled at his apologies and went right to work. After Homer had brought in firewood she handed him the milk bucket saying gaily, "It's no use pretending to me that you've milked. I know better."

After dinner, while Ann was still busy in the kitchen, Homer called from the front window, "Miss Ann, do come and see this."

"What is it—more settlers going west?" she asked lightly.

"No, it's an ox cart coming into town, and I can't make out what the fellow is hauling. There's something covered up with a buffalo robe, stretched out on some hay in the bottom."

Ann hurried from the kitchen, wiping her hands as she went.

"Why, it's that Mr. Howe! That's little Charley standing in the back of the cart."

"But what is he hauling? I never saw Ben's cattle walk that slow."

"Oh, don't you see, it's Laura there in that awful cart. He's bringing her to town—Julia Goodell offered to care for her if he would just bring her there."

Slowly the big ungainly cart passed, its great wheels rumbling and creaking over the half-frozen ruts of the stage road. Ben Howe walking beside his cattle tugged often at the gee line to slow their gait.

Ann stood at the window until the cart disappeared beyond the cluster of buildings on Main Street.

Chapter 8

As Ann pushed open the door of the darkened kitchen, Doshia called to her, "You're late tonight, child. How are Amelia and the twins?"

"Oh, they are all right," Ann replied a bit wearily. "I did a big washing, then baked bread while I had the stove hot for the sadirons. Where is everybody?"

"Oh, they all went to singing school—even Philo."

"Singing school! Oh dear, I forgot about it—and I'd promised to go."

"Probably Amelia needed you worse than the singing school."

"I could have hurried a little faster, if I'd remembered."

"It's too bad—it would have done you good."

An hour later Philo and her brothers returned gaily. "Gee, sis, you should have been there," Stan said.

"I know—I'd promised to go."

"If it was your friend Lucy Bigsby you'd promised, she wouldn't have missed you anyway—she was busy and stepping high tonight. A new man in town."

"What difference would that make to her?" Ann asked innocently.

Emery laughed.

"Same as every likely young stranger in town affects her. She brought this one a songbook and even found the page for him!"

"And who is the newcomer?" Ann asked casually.

"A fellow name of Will Benton down Maine somewhere—starting a carpenter shop down by Clack's mill," Stan explained.

"I heard Henry Laurie sidle over to this Benton and give him the lowdown on Miss Lucy," Emery laughed. "He told him to duck and run soon as singing school let out, or he'd get elected to walk her home."

"Then Henry was there tonight," Ann said simply.

"Sure was, and having a lot of fun—he walked up the road with us as far as Forbes. We asked him to come in and talk a while but he said he would come over some other time."

"He seems so bashful," Doshia observed.

"But he's getting over that. Why he even asked where you were, sis."

Stephen interrupted with, "Now, if you are ready—" and reached for the Bible. That night he again remembered Laura Howe in his prayer. "We ask for Thy Divine Help for this woman in our midst who struggles for life this very hour."

It was several days before Ann saw Henry Laurie again, and then it was in the store under Anor's watchful eye.

"I missed seeing you at singing school, Miss Ann—I hope you weren't sick—or anything," he murmured questioningly.

"I had to stay late at Hanlons that evening."

"I was going to walk home with you—I had something to talk to you about," he said in a low tone Anor could not hear.

"We could have had a nice visit," she said in a matter-of-fact tone. "Do come over most any evening—the boys and Philo are always home—and I'll stop knitting to make popcorn for you folks."

"I promised to tell your fortune—remember?"

"Oh, yes, Henry, that would be fun to hear. Don't forget how it's going to be."

"It can wait, Miss Ann. I'll never forget it—ever."

Ten days later, Mrs. Bigsby called at the Barretts and as she was leaving, invited Ann and Philo to supper on Friday. "Come for early supper, and then you girls and my Lucy can walk to singing school together. Lucy is real anxious to go, though, land sakes, I never know how she will get home again. I hate to ask her father to go after her."

Philo suppressed a giggle.

In the early dark of the fall evening, the three young women hurried along the trace of the stage road back to the colony. To the right of the road the lights of Bert and Susan Hillman's new little house twinkled cheerily. To the left nearer town, the Reverend Lorimer's house stood alone on the prairie, marked now by a flurry of fine sparks drifting up from the stovepipe like a sudden flight of fireflies on a summer night.

As the three crossed the park in front of Goodell's new house, lights shone from both front windows. Ann stopped and said in a low tone, "I'm afraid it's something about Laura Howe. She is sick there in Julia's parlor room. But it's all lighted up now."

"There is someone walking back and forth outside," Philo whispered. "I saw him pass the window, and he looks too tall to be Mr. Goodell."

Miss Lucy started on ahead.

"We must hurry—I've got to be there to pass out the songbooks."

As they entered the schoolroom, Emery came up. "It's sad news about Ben's wife. She died about dusk. Sarah Phipps sent word to mother to come help her, but she isn't able. Sarah is down there now laying out Laura and getting her dressed."

The news of Laura Howe's death put a restraint on the merriment that evening. Gideon Jardine selected none of the rollicking, popular tunes the young people enjoyed. After all, the Howes were neighbors of the Jardines, besides living pretty close to town and being members of the First Church, too. Ann Barrett sang along with the rest, but her heart was not in it.

Word passed around town the next day that Julia Goodell had offered to have the funeral at her house right after dinner on the Sabbath. Ben, bewildered and stricken, had gladly accepted. Will Benton offered to make the pine box, and Julia Goodell and Sarah offered to line it. After Julia gave one of her old silk dresses for the purpose.

That same afternoon, Emery, with Henry Hillman and Jim Harrison's oldest boy, tossed shovels into a wagon and drove out to Ben's farm. He had insisted that Laura be buried right there in the garden beside her baby.

The sun was low in the west when they had finished, and in the deeper hollows the darkening haze of approaching dusk was already forming. A chill wind rattled the dry bean stems in the garden and stirred the dead leaves of Ben's corn patch, sending wisps of blades drifting falteringly across the garden to mingle with the fresh-dug clods as if to hide the stark bareness of the mound. High above, a long wavering V of wild ducks winged southward.

"Sure sign of winter coming," young Harrison remarked, cleaning his shovel.

At two o'clock on the Sabbath, the Reverend Goodell conducted services for Laura in his own parlor. While Ben had not expected many, Julia had been foresighted and had the furniture set outdoors and planks laid across blocks of wood. Indoors it was mostly women, with a few of the older men who did not relish standing in the cold.

After the simple service folks stood outside, waiting backs to the wind, 'till the pine box was placed in Jim Harrison's wagon for the trip out to the ridge beyond town. Ben, more haggard and gaunt than ever, climbed into the buggy with the minister and they drove away ahead of the wagon.

That night Ann included little Charley in her prayers, as she had done for some time. And afterwards she wondered why she was sharing the grief of a small boy and of the man she scarcely knew.

Chapter 9

Several weeks passed before any of the Barretts saw Ben Howe again. Meantime Ann kept posted as best she could regarding the four-year-old. From Julia Goodell she learned that Ben insisted on taking Charley back to the cabin, rather than allow Julia or anyone to add the boy to their own flock.

One Sabbath morning early in December, as the family were getting ready for meeting, Philo called to Ann, "Oh, look, here comes your widower friend, Mr. Howe, on his way to meeting."

"He is nothing to me," Ann replied, calmly tying the long ribbons of her brown satin bonnet before joining her sister at the window. "It's the little fellow who is my special friend."

"That little brat!" Philo replied tartly.

"Poor motherless little fellow—" Ann murmured, as she watched Charley hopping along over the light snow his little legs fairly flying to keep pace with his father's hurried strides.

"If you'd ask me," Philo said haughtily, "the old goat isn't likely to find any woman in this town willing to marry him and raise that brat besides."

Stephen stepped into the room just then and said firmly, "Daughter, you must never speak so thoughtlessly of anyone in trouble." Turning to Doshia, he added, "That's the trouble," nodding toward Philo, "she is too old to spank and not old enough to know better."

When the Barretts arrived, Ben had already taken a seat in the back of the schoolroom and nodded casually to Stephen. Little Charley was showing new boots to those who sat near. Once, as he came down the aisle, Ann spoke his name and put out an arm as if to draw him to her. But the child slipped away and displayed the boots from a safe distance, pointing to their bright red leather tops and shiney copper-covered toes.

As the child clumped up and down the aisle, Ann scanned his face and figure for sign of neglect. Once his face lighted with a wan smile as he looked at her. Vaguely she wondered if Gerty's prediction would come true. Mr. Howe did not appear much concerned about the child.

After meeting, Gideon Jardine hurried back from his choir sitting on the front row, to seek out Ann. He began, clearing his throat in evident embarrassment, "I have a favor to ask of you—we are—I mean my son's wife—is expecting to be confined real soon— and we've been hoping you could come to help a few days—when it happens. Homer Hanlon says you are such good help." Then he added, "I'll come and get you myself."

In early December, Emery Barrett took the stage at Latmeier's on the first lap of his journey back to New Hampshire. Hannah Stover had waited long enough to become his bride.

Two weeks later, at midnight, the newlyweds stepped down from the stage at George Chapin's tavern right in the middle of Goodell. Hannah, a trusting and adoring bride, felt sure that Emery had planned all that week-long trip for their arrival on the day the stage came through town instead of their being dumped out at Latmeier's four miles away.

Loaded with hand luggage the young couple came directly to Stephen's to occupy one corner of the low-ceilinged, unplastered upstairs until their new house down by Clack's mill was ready. In the wan light of Stephen's candle held high in the doorway, Hannah Barrett looked strangely young and tiny beside her tall, bearded husband. She was not handsome. Peculiarly slanting eyebrows, set high on a bony forehead, gave her a constant quizzical look. Her nose was too long to add anything to her appearance.

At breakfast the next morning the Barretts sat much longer than usual to hear, mostly from Hannah, the news of the old neighborhood. Boisterous Stan interspersed the talk with sly jibes at the bride and groom, despite his parents.

Hannah kept up her running account of their wedding and of their wedding trip west. She loved to talk, especially to appreciative listeners.

"Of course we came on the steam cars as far as the Mississippi," she continued gaily, "and then we had to cross on the ice—"

"Just like Eliza in that slavery story?" Stan asked impishly.

"No, we rode in a bobsled," she said firmly. "When we got to Davenport we had to wait half a day for the steam cars to take us to the end of the line—so we went and bought ourselves a wedding present. Dear, run upstairs and bring those silver teaspoons."

"Gee, Hannah, don't ask him to go wasting his strength like going upstairs till we get that load of hay, today," Stan pleaded.

"We thought we should have something besides our fancy wedding certificate," Emery said jocularly, turning away from Stan. "I'm going to frame that and hang it in our bedroom."

"You folks had a long wedding trip!" Ann exclaimed. "By rail, by bobsled, by rail again, and then by stage! Now when I get married—ahem—I expect a real nice fashionable wedding trip in an ox cart, and nothing so speedy as the steam cars for me!"

She joined in the laughter and Stan said, "She has been saying that ever since I can remember."

Stephen pushed back from the table and went abruptly to the window. In a minute he cut short Hannah's account with, "It looks like there's a change in the weather coming. You boys better get that load of hay from the stack out there. The one Stan has been joking about."

Long before nightfall the wind shifted to the north and rose to gale strength, bringing with it new snow blown in horizontal sheets. Hanlon's farmhouse, scarce a quarter of a mile away, was the first to be blotted from sight, and, as the wind and snow increased, even the long cabin and Shute's store disappeared as if lifted away by some giant hand. The hollow roar of the storm drowned out all other sounds save the whine and whistle of some loose sliver in the unpainted siding, a whine that rose and fell in tone with the gusts of wind.

Emery, restless and fearful for the cows and horses, finally slipped into his boots and motioned to Stan.

"You've got to stay together," Stephen warned nervously. "Get that coil of rope you lash down your freight with—it's in the lean-to—and tie to the pump and pay it out behind till you find the stable. Lol Phipps says it's the only way."

Stephen and the womanfolk stood anxiously at the window as the two men, muffled and bundled in coats and scarves, made fast the rope and dropped from sight into the welter of the storm. For a time the rope jerked spasmodically on the pump, then lay still.

"They've stopped walking," Stephen said uneasily.

The others who watched knew very well the doubt his tone expressed. Had the two reached the stable—had Emery lost hold of the rope, or had the two become separated?

"Lol says if—"

"If you repeat another word that man says about this awful—country—I'll scream!"

"Now mother," Stephen reassured her, "don't worry about the boys. Emery won't stray out on the prairie and get lost."

"What will he do—walk in circles till they freeze to death?"

"They are grown men, mother. Look at Hannah here—calm as can be—aren't you, my dear?"

The girl smiled fleetingly up at him but said nothing.

After an interval that seemed hours, the slender rope tugged three times on the pump.

"Look there. I told you, mother, we had nothing to worry about. That's the signal they've reached the stable."

Doshia smiled wanly as she turned from the window, saying, "Honest, Stephen Barrett, I don't see how you can change so fast."

Ann stood at the window after the others had moved away, thinking, What is little Charley doing—is he watching for his father to come back from their stable? What would happen if Mr. Howe didn't get back?

Thirty-six hours later the colony awakened to find a dazzling white world, strangely silent now the storm had blown itself out. Huge drifts lay in the lee of every building, and some were almost buried.

Time had stood still as the days and nights merged during the sotrm, so it was not surprising that Christmas passed unnoticed.

Three days later, Gideon Jardine came with team and sled to fetch Ann as planned. Hurrying to pack she thought happily, if he pays me even fifty cents a day like Mr. Hanlon did, I'll have enough to send for that five-drawer dresser Emery saw in Iowa City his last trip.

It was the second Sabbath, and late afternoon, when Gideon brought her home. She hopped out of the sled, happy to be home again and proud to have seven whole dollars in her small beaded purse.

As Ann crowded into the kitchen, her mother kissed her and then, glancing around mysteriously, said, "We have a surprise for you, child, something new. And we are glad to have you home to help us enjoy it."

"But he couldn't have gotten it yet," Ann stammered, "he couldn't have been to Iowa City in this weather—or leave Hannah," she said and laughed.

"No, it's nothing from the city," Doshia assured her. "You'd never guess."

Ann looked past them into the sitting room. Little Charley Howe stood beside Philo, waiting. Ann ran forward, holding out her arms to him. The child hesitated only a minute, repeating questioningly, "Mommie—Mommie." Then he ran and put his arms around her neck.

Ann's eyes shone as she looked up to her mother, past the boy's tousled head and murmured, "For a moment he thought I was his m-o-t-h-e-r, coming in this way and with my wraps on. Isn't he sweet—and sad?"

To the child she said softly, "Can you say Aunt Ann?" He tried the strange new words over and over and put a hand to each side of her face while he seemed to be studying her features.

"Looks like I've lost my small admirer already," Philo said with unusual cheerfulness, and Charley pulled away and ran to her begging, "Lift me way up, Aunt Pilo."

No one even thought of going to meeting that evening. The women were clearing up the kitchen when there was a knock on the door. Ann opened it to find Ben Howe standing in the circle of light.

"I just stopped by from meeting to see how the boy is, ma'am."

"Yes, of course. Do come in. Here is the bootjack—just set them behind the stove."

Ben joined Stephen and Emery in the sitting room and held little Charley on his lap until Ann came to carry the boy off to his bed beside her own. Very manfully, he kissed all his aunts, and his father last of all. From the bedroom Ann could be heard prompting him in the prayer Hannah had begun teaching him.

When she returned to the sitting room, Stephen reached for the Bible and began his usual prayer service. When it was over, he rose and excused himself, saying, "It is a trifle early, but I believe I'll retire." One by one the others drifted away to bed until only Ann and Ben remained. He seemed very comfortable in the pleasant warmth of the cheerful room and made no move to go home. Ann kept on knitting.

Conversation lagged. Finally Ben cleared his throat nervously. "It was good of you folks to take the boy to board," he said in a melancholy tone.

"Mother always does what she can for people who need help." Ann looked up from her knitting, but Ben's gaze was on the firelight in the heating stove and not upon her.

"I could see he needed a woman's hand and a hand to train him—like learning him his prayers, for instance. She was a good woman, Laura was. I'll never forget her."

Ann nodded agreement as she said in a low tone, "Of course you will not forget her."

"Well, she's been dead two months now," Ben said easily.

There was another silence while Ann tried to think of some way to lead the talk to more pleasant subjects. Two months now.

"Have you been to the river towns lately, Mr. Howe?" she asked brightly.

"Oh no, Miss Ann, you see I don't own narry a horse."

"Then you haven't been to Iowa City either?"

"Oh, no. Why?"

"I wondered if you knew any more about the new railroad—whether they got the first train into the city before New Year's to get that big reward."

"Well, yes, I did hear some talk about it at Shute's store. Henry Laurie was laughing about the steam engine freezing up that last evening just a few minutes before midnight—and how they had to push it and one car the last hundred yards over track they'd just laid. Maybe you know more about it than I do from hearsay. Miss Ann, Isn't that a stack of *Iowa City Gazettes* there?"

Ann stammered, "Yes, they are, but—well, I haven't been home to read them, you see."

"I heard at meeting this evening you'd just come home."

She tried another subject. "Henry Laurie was telling me not long ago that you came here about the same time he did—when Mr. Goodell first started the colony."

A shadow crossed Ben's bewhiskered face. "Yes, I bunked with Henry in the long cabin across the road here, soon as we got it built. Later, after Emery came, the three of us slept up over Shute's store with Anor and his wife and the hired girl."

"He never mentioned that, Mr. Howe."

"I am glad, because Henry is such a joker he would leave out telling there was a calico curtain across the loft, Miss Ann."

Ann suppressed a giggle and managed to say, "Of course there was a curtain, Mr. Howe."

The sound of the big clock on the wall striking ten brought Ben to his senses. He made good pretenses of his surprise at how late it really was, and headed for the kitchen. Ann followed with the candle. Standing by the door, he apologized again, then bade her good night and hurried away.

Ann moved quietly across the house to her bedroom and stood looking down at Charley. Now he is here where I can look after him, like I've wanted to for so long. After a full minute, she stealthily took down her diary from the shelf and returned to the low rocker by the fire. There was so much to write down. She sat puzzling for several minutes before she took up the tablet and wrote rapidly, "January 13, 1856. Received Mr. Howe's company."

Chapter 10

Ben Howe did his chores very early the following Thursday, ate a bite of supper, and started afoot to prayer meeting, glad to leave the cluttered cabin with its greasy cooking smells.

Friends greeted him warmly when he entered the schoolroom. To his relief, no one seemed surprised to see him there. Henry Laurie came over, smiling as usual and, as he shook hands, said cordially, "I see your boy over at Barrett's quite often. I noticed the other night he is getting heavier."

Miss Debbie Hart turned clear around to say, "We are all so happy you found such a nice place for Charley to stay—temporary, of course. As I always say, it takes a woman's hand."

When the prayer service was over, Ben sought out Stephen and Doshia and said earnestly, "I do hope the boy isn't sick. I noticed Miss Ann nor the other young ladies are here. I think, sir, that I'd better go by and stop to see him."

"He is real well," Doshia assured him. "With all of us waiting on him, he doesn't have time to be lonesome."

As they waited for Ben at the door, Stephen whispered, "It's strange his taking such a sudden interest in the boy—he didn't show up at all for most two weeks after he brought him to us."

When they entered the Barrett kitchen, Ann greeted Ben with genuine surprise and added, "I know you wanted to see Charley, but he's just gone to sleep—but we have some popcorn left."

"I thought I'd just stop by to see him and see if he needed anything," Ben said.

Ann suppressed a smile. It was word for word what he had said last Sabbath. She picked up a candle, saying pleasantly, "You will want to see him, even if he is asleep."

As she bent over the sleeping child and tucked the quilt

carefully about his shoulders, Ben said huskily, "Miss Ann, seeing him here so well tended and safe—I can't explain how I appreciate you doing all this for me."

"Mother is always glad to help people in need," she hastened to say, without looking up.

Back in the sitting room, Stephen read from the Bible and prayed. Then, turning to Ann, he asked, "How about a wedge of that hot mince pie for Ben and me? You will have a piece, won't you, sir?"

"Don't care if I do. Haven't had a pie since—"

Stephen interrupted with, "I do like pie before retiring."

Ben had scarcely tasted his piece when he said eagerly, "I dare say you made this wonderful pie, Miss Ann?"

"Why, no. This is one of a batch mother and the girls baked while I was at Jardine's. They keep frozen you know. Mother puts some in the warming oven every night during the winter so father can have some."

She was yawning, thinking of another long evening of knitting— and visiting alone with Mr. Howe.

Early Saturday evening, Jim Harrison's oldest boy came across the townsite with team and bobsled, picking up young folks for a ride out to the settlement on Sugar Creek. As he stopped at Barrett's the sleigh bells were silent till all five of them were bundled close together on the deep mat of prairie hay beneath buffalo robes. Then they were off down the road to Deacon Forbes's new house. Henry Laurie came running out and caught onto the sled.

"You saving a place for me, Miss Ann?" he asked, pulling at the robe.

"You are too fat to get in that space," young Harrison warned.

"All the more of me to love," Henry said and chuckled. "Isn't that right, Ann?"

"Oh, I'm sorry, but I wasn't listening."

"Where was your mind wandering, young lady?"

"Wouldn't you like to know," she bantered.

After the last of the passengers had been picked up, the sled headed west on the stage road toward the Sugar Creek ford. "Anybody know how far it is to Rose's cabin?" someone asked.

"Four miles," Henry Laurie piped up, "and I should know from the times I've walked it. I'd have you children know I cut the logs for that very cabin the spring of '54."

Maria Rose was standing in the door of the cabin as the sled stopped. "Come in," she called cheerily. "I heard you folks were acoming. So I've got both dish pans full of popcorn already. And the boys drew molasses from the barrel for pull candy."

Catching sight of Ann, she exclaimed, "I was a hopin' you'd come with the young folks! My Bob and me never will forget how your ma and pa took us when we landed at the colony in that wind and rain storm. What do you find to do these days, young lady—and how are the old folks?"

"Oh, haven't you heard—we have had Ben Howe's little boy at our house ever since New Year's. Mr. Howe brought him to mother while I was at Jardine's helping with the new baby."

"I'd heard about the baby, but I didn't know you folks had Ben's young'un."

"We have him for now anyway," Ann said with a sigh. "He is such a sweet little fellow—and the way he clings to me, like tonight when I came away. It breaks my heart thinking Mr. Howe will likely be taking him home come spring."

Above the sound of merriment within the cabin, Maria said shrewdly, "Seems to me it would be better if Ben got somebody to take the boy for a while. He will like as not marry again, if he can find some woman to put up with his tantrums."

"Oh, Maria, Charley doesn't have tantrums."

"I mean old Ben himself. If he is bound to git married again, he ought to get somebody like Debbie Hart. She wouldn't take any of his foolishness."

"But maybe Miss Debbie—or somebody like that—wouldn't be good to Charley."

"You can mark my word, young lady, all boys that age and older are whippersnappers and need a strong hand."

When the two women reentered the main room of the cabin the party was in full swing with the girls stirring the molasses, boiling for pull candy, and the boys making popcorn disappear, washed down with mugs of cold milk. Later, when the molasses candy was cool enough to pull, Henry Laurie came to Ann with a rope of the brownish-yellow stuff. Hand over hand, they pulled and doubled and pulled until it was firm. Once, as he stood facing her, grinning, she warned him, "Quit watching me or you'll drop our candy!"

"You look so happy. You're having fun, aren't you, Ann?"

"Yes, of course," she said in a low tone, her eyes laughing.

"Come, let's get a tin pan and set it outdoors to cool."

He closed the heavy door behind him as she hurried to set the pan in the snowbank. She turned quickly, and his arms went about her and he whispered, "I've been trying all evening to see any encouragement in your pretty brown eyes, you merry little iceberg—and now I can see it plain as day—you do care for me."

He pressed hard against her and felt her body relax in his arms. Looking down into her eyes, he murmured softly, "You knew all along that I loved you."

"Oh, Henry, I do care about you—but—" As she faltered, he felt her heart beating faster. "I never felt this way—before—about anyone—but I've got to have time to think."

"Please don't say I'm a week too late," he begged.

"Oh, Henry, It's so hard to know what I want to do—I have to think of—others."

"And throw yourself away?"

The cabin door opened, and young Harrison called out, "Hey, you two, what is going on out here?"

"Just setting the candy out to cool. Let's go in, Ann."

Later, on the way home in the sled she was silent a long time, warm beneath the robes beside Henry. She was trying to think, but the image of little Charley kept bobbing up. She tried shutting her eyes to the crisp white worls of reality around her, but his piping little voice calling, "Aunt Ann, come here, I need you" rang in her ears above the monotone of muffled voices nearby and the squeak of the sled runners on the hard-packed snow.

As the sled began to climb the long hill toward the colony, the moon rose full and clear, casting weird shadows on the snow. Across the valley a worried farm dog barked frantically to challenge a coyote call.

"That's his sod cabin over there, Ann," Henry murmured close to her ear. "It's no place for a woman like you—over there." He pointed a mittened hand to a cluster of shadowy objects across the valley. "You'd be throwing yourself away—with him."

"Why do you say that, Henry?" she stammered. "Is that my fortune you are telling?"

"I was going to tell you about your future—with me," he said in a low tone, "but I didn't think there was any hurry—that you'd be interested in hin."

"But Henry—I never once thought—"

"I want to be somebody and get ahead in the world—not always work in a general store—I'm putting money in land, planning ahead for you and me, Ann."

She turned and looked into his face that was so serious now, close against her shoulder, and murmured, "I'll never forget tonight, Henry, whatever happens to me."

At home, in the pleasant warmth of the sitting room, she tarried long after the rest had gone to bed. With her diary in her lap she sat in the low rocker staring into the dying flames of the wood fire. Almost sadly she thought, tomorrow is the Sabbath and Mr. Howe is bound to stop by again.

Stephen invited Ben home to dinner after meeting the next day. Ann felt relieved when she saw him coming up the path, for at least he wouldn't stay so long and I wouldn't have to entertain him. She was busy in the kitchen both before and after dinner, and Ben went home at midafternoon to do his chores.

On Thursday evening he stopped by as usual after prayer meeting. Again, one by one the family went off to bed, leaving Ann alone with the visitor. Her knitting was progressing rapidly of late, with so many evenings devoted to it.

It had been a mild winter day, but half an hour before ten o'clock the wind changed. It grew colder in the sitting room, and Ben got up and put wood in the fire but sat down again. After a few minutes he said earnestly, "I declare, Miss Ann, it is so pleasant here."

"We think it's rather nice. Father was anxious to make it as comfortable as the house back East."

"Take my cabin for instance—" he began.

"Mr. Howe, isn't that snow beating against the window?"

One glance from the kitchen door showed a world of swirling, driving snow. "I'll not let you start afoot in this storm. You must think of little Charley as well as yourself. You might get lost on the prairie and never find your cabin. No, you'll stay right here."

"But, ma'am, I think I'd better go to George Chapin's tavern."

"Father wouldn't hear of you paying fifty cents for a place to sleep."

So, fully dressed except for his boots, Ben went to bed on the floor of the unfinished back room upstairs, covered with a buffalo robe and a quilt.

Ann lay a long time in her bed looking up in the dark, thinking.

What shall I do about that man—upstairs. Why, I hardly know him. And the wind shrieking around the house, lulled her to sleep before she could ponder an answer.

The following Sabbath, Ben intercepted her at the close of the early candlelight service and said, "I'll walk up the path with you, if you don't mind."

He took her arm graciously and babbled rather nervously about nothing all the way to Stephen's. Part way, he stepped back in passing someone in the dark. Ann recognized Henry Laurie and sang out cheerily, "Meeting is all over! Won't you come over to the house for a while? I'll make some popcorn for both of you."

Henry paused only long enough to say, "No thanks, Ann, I'm too worried about a claim jumper."

After he passed, Ben said reprovingly, "I was surprised that you called him by his first name. It was nice of you to ask him over. I didn't know he had a claim—must be some of that new land in Jason County."

"I think it is a claim he never got around to file for," she said mysteriously.

"A man has to watch out for himself to get ahead nowadays," Ben said confidentially.

After the rest of the family had gone to bed, Ben seemed more talkative than usual. All he needed from Ann was a nod of assent or a question or two, and he was off again on some long-drawn tale. It was quite plain that he was rapidly coming to the point when he led the conversation, one-sided though it was, to the merits of his eighty acres.

"I guess I've told you, Miss Ann, I had ten acres of prairie broke in the fall of '54—that's how I got the sod to lay the cabin walls. You see I was fixin' for Laura and the boy to come out from the East. Well, ma'am, come spring I got the corn planted—all alone, too—and I never touched it from planting to harvest—just let her grow, and she made twenty bushels to an acre!"

"I know the planting is hard work, chopping a slit with an ax for each hill."

"Yes, ma'am, but I got it done alone, that is, except when Charley dropped seed for me a day or so."

"But Charley was so little away last spring—how could he?"

"I had to urge him quite a bit, but he did right well after that—and my wheat," he babbled on, "I put in two acres and it made thirty bushels—keep us in flour quite a spell."

"That was nice," Ann said without looking up from the knitting.

"I'm getting a nice herd of cattle started—I aim to graze them on the open prairie over in Jason County—and come fall I'll have several to sell and one for us to butcher, besides."

Ann had followed all this talk with only mild interest until Ben began using words "us" and "our." She tried to assure herself that he was only talking that way to say he would be taking Charley home with him, come spring.

There was a brief silence while the wood in the stove crackled and a big chunk burned away and settled in the firebox. Ben, sitting drumming his fingers on the arm of the hickory chair, moved uneasily and cleared his throat. Ann was tempted to ask if he had a cold.

"I'm aiming to tear the sod off the cabin frame come summer, Miss Ann. I want to put on real siding—like your father's here, lay a real board floor and lath and plaster it all."

He paused to give her time to appreciate his plans.

"And if we do right well I aim to build on a pantry. Women like pantries."

Ann never stopped knitting. She was certain now that his use of the plural pronouns was no slip of the tongue. He continued to clear his throat.

"I've been thinking a lot about us lately," he began.

Ann put down her knitting so quickly the ball of yarn rolled off her lap and across the floor. She started to retrieve it, but Ben was going on in the same matter-of-fact tone as though bargaining for groceries. "I've been thinking about our future."

Future, she thought wildly—Henry was going to foretell mine.

"I'm pretty lonesome out there since Laura went—and with Charley gone."

"Of course you are, Mr. Howe," she murmured, stalling.

"I've been thinking I could have the boy at home like he should be, if you'd consent to come out and be my wife."

It was as simple as that. He had not stirred from his chair on the opposite side of the stove. Indecision gripped her. As she wavered, Ben turned his gaze from the stove toward the door of the bedroom where little Charley lay asleep. Desperately she thought, I do love him so—this way I'd never have to give him up, never.

Demurely she folded her hands and looked up, smiling happily now that all doubt was gone. "Yes, Mr. Howe, I will be pleased to marry you."

"Well, that's fine. I was hoping you'd see it that way," he said loftily settling back in his chair.

Ann retrieved her own ball of yarn and began knitting, albeit without her usual speed or precision.

When the clock struck ten, Ben looked up as if to assure himself the strike was correct. "I declare I didn't know it was so late, Ann — I'll call you that now. Likely I'll stop by again after prayer meeting Thursday and we can decide more — about this."

She picked up the candle and led the way to the kitchen, but promptly set the light down, thinking, if he does want to kiss me I shouldn't be holding this.

Ben put on his boots, buttoned his heavy frock and strode rapidly to the door. As he passed, she caught his sleeve and murmured, "Do be careful of yourself till I see you again, Mr. Howe."

As he went down the steps he called back, "I'll do that. And you take good care of Charley."

Ann returned to the empty sitting room, not knowing whether to be sad or happy. She went to get down her diary and sat rereading the one penciled page that told it all. Then, without emotion, she wrote, "Jan. 27. — Mr. Howe came. We engaged."

Chapter 11

Ben's thoughts were running riot that night as he walked rapidly across the townsite and out onto the prairie toward home. *I've done right well by myself—getting tied up with old Deacon Barrett's daughter, the belle of the town. This will make folks talk. Me getting married again so quick. They'll be thinking it's on account of Charley, but he is all right where he is now. Likely she'll be a little skittish at first, but they say an old maid makes a good bedfellow.*

At the door of his cabin Ben paused, reluctant to enter. He remembered his own hasty departure that had left a clutter worse than usual. He pushed open the heavy door, and the stale smell of old potato peelings and greasy skillets rushed to meet him. The cookstove fire had long since burned out, and already a damp chill was penetrating the thick walls. *It would be nice to snug up to a woman again.*

Smiling at the thought, he picked up the candle and entered the tiny bedroom from the kitchen. The unmade bed held a clutter of work clothes which he dumped on the hard dirt floor. Removing only his boots and heavy frock, he climbed between the blankets.

The following Thursday Ben stopped at Barrett's after prayer meeting as usual. Ann had not attended, thinking, *if I'm not there it won't look like I'm running after him—and maybe he has changed his mind.*

As soon as they were alone, Ben began talking about the wedding. "I think we should be married right away," he said with noticeable firmness.

"But Mr. Howe, I can't possibly be ready before April or May. I have not told the family yet, and besides father wants me to make him a pair of pants. It bothers mother so to do it."

"I don't want a big showy wedding, account of Laura and all."

"But Mr. Howe, I don't know how I could invite just a few.

There are so many I'd want to come—the Harrisons, the Phipps, the Holts, and the Hanlons and Shutes of course. Oh, and lots of others," she said and laughed.

"Well, as I was saying, I'm real anxious to get it done right away. I guess you wouldn't know why—never being married," and he smiled faintly. "It would be a lot better for me to have the wedding before heavy spring work begins."

"Shall we set the date, Mr. Howe?"

"Yes, and I favor a Sabbath evening right after meetin' this time of year. Folks would mostly be there, and besides it would save heating up the schoolhouse just for us to get married."

"I'm pretty sure mother would want to have a real nice reception after the—ceremony," she went on animatedly, "just like she had for Hannah and Emery—with nice refreshments and all."

She reached for the almanac that lay on the stand beside the candleholder. As she handed it to him, she touched his rough hairy arm, and she drew back quickly, leaving him the pamphlet open to March.

She managed to say, "Do read their conjecture for the weather on the 26th, Mr. Howe. It says it will be bright and sunny. Wouldn't that be a wonderful day for our wedding?"

"I guess that will do," he replied without enthusiasm, thumbing back into February. "I'd like it to be on the Sabbath, though it wouldn't make so much difference, just so it's after sundown. I'd be too busy during the day, that close to spring."

He looked at her closely and moistened his lips. *Too bad she has so much gettin' ready to do, just to get married.*

"Oh I'm so proud to be your wife." She laughed gaily. "And now I'll be Charley's real mother for always."

"I wouldn't say that, Ann. There will always be Laura. We can't forget her, his own mother."

"I do love him like he was really ours. And now I won't ever have to give him up. I'd worried you might take him away."

"Why, I never even thought of that!"

"Oh," she said dully, hoping he had not noticed her dismay.

At times during the first days and weeks of her engagement, Ann felt real elation at the prospect of becoming Mrs. Ben Howe. At such times she would smile to herself. *It's wonderful to be loved—and little Charley needs me so.* Again, doubts would creep into her thinking. *Does he really love me—he seems so matter of fact about* everything. And when I look at those hairy arms I believe I'd scream if he put them around me."

True to her promise to Stephen, his woolen breeches were finished before Ann and her mother even took stock of her trousseau.

"Here is the deep wine color silk," Doshia announced from the depths of the closet, "and it is such a nice dress—have you thought about that?"

"No. I guess I thought I had to have a new one." She hesitated before adding, "Though I've hardly had time to think about anything."

"But child, do be sensible. Ben is in very close circumstances. You are going to live in the country, and anyway the silk is beautiful. Look at all the yards and yards of braid—and then the velvet trim—and those side panniers are still right in style according to *Godey's.*"

"It does look nice," Ann admitted readily. "I guess I haven't worn it but once in Goodell, and that was at Susan Harrison's wedding."

So, without any real disappointment to Ann, it was decided she would be married in the wine-colored silk. At once the dress took on new charm and significance. "My wedding dress—mine," she would whisper as she fingered its folds, in disbelief that she was to be a bride.

On his next trip to Muscatine, Emery carried one of Ann's twenty-dollar gold pieces and a list of her needs. Returning ten days later, delayed by storms, he brought all that she had asked for, and five dollars in change.

"You cheated yourself," she told him, gaily opening the boxes and checking the list. "It comes to fifteen forty-two."

"I've got something extra for you, sis. It's on the wagon. I brought a new bureau for you—and one for Hannah. I looked all over Iowa City, and these were the last two. I hope they didn't get scratched—I had to tie them on top of my load."

Most important of all the packages from the river was the special box in which lay the wedding bonnet.

"Oh isn't it lovely," Ann gasped, lifting it up for all to see. "To think that Emery picked it out for me. A white velvet bonnet will surprise a lot of folks in this town. Susan Hillman said the other day she supposed I'd have one to match my wine dress."

"What luscious white velvet," Philo said as she held it up and turned it around. "The off-the-face model is the very latest. *Godey's*

Lady's Book says they are being worn farther back on the head this year. And this little quilted rool of satin around the front will frame your face so sweet, Ann."

Standing before the mirror, Ann looked in amazement at the person reflected there. Ann Barrett in a wedding bonnet!

On the infrequent nights his father called, Charley was invariably well mannered. At other times he was a noisy, stubborn little rascal whose tantrums worried Ann greatly.

"You three girls are spoiling him," Doshia warned. "But likely with Mr. Howe's help you can straighten him out. It's a wonder he isn't worse than he is—losing his mother and being moved around. I hope Mr. Howe isn't planning to move you and Charley out to the farm right away."

"He hasn't said much about Charley," Ann admitted quietly, "but he plans to move me and my baggage right away. He wanted me to move my furniture and even my clothes out to his cabin before the wedding."

"Well, I'm glad you would not let him," Doshia sighed. "You can't be too careful about appearances. How it would look if one of you died and your clothes were in his house!"

"Oh please, mother, don't talk about death when life for me is just beginning."

"I do hope you will be happy, child—but the lot of a married woman isn't always easy. A husband is oftentimes just like a man—demanding his rights, and it's a woman's duty to submit."

Doshia sighed thoughtfully and shook her head.

Guests began arriving well before seven o'clock, some invited by word-of-mouth, while others, seeing the schoolhouse lighted, just stopped by.

Ben arrived on foot long before the ceremony, looking quite spruce. He was wearing a good-looking suit, a trifle tight, a new white dickey over a much washed flannel shirt whose sleeves showed badly when he raised his arms. A string tie, black wool hat and freshly greased boots completed his attire.

A few minutes before seven, Stephen came out on the steps of the schoolhouse and asked anxiously, "Ben, has the minister come?"

"Likely he is indoors there waiting," he answered easily.

"By chance did you forget to engage him?"

"No, I spoke to him long ago. I remember I had to make a special trip to see him."

Stephen turned and called Stan from a group nearby. "Here, take this lantern and go get Reverend Lorimer, quick."

Jim Harrison's oldest boy laughed loudly and called out, "Sounds like he was afraid the groom would run off if he had to wait."

Stephen came to the door every few minutes to peer out for sight of the lantern returning, but it was fully twenty minutes before the elderly minister arrived quite out of breath. "My apologies to you, Deacon Barrett, and to you, Mr. Howe. I declare this ceremony had completely slipped my mind. I had retired for the night."

From the dark a voice called out, "Hey Ben, follow the old gent's advice and go to bed early!"

Young Harrison took up the teasing again with, "Ben will likely spend most of the spring in bed or leastwise in the house. We'll have to go help him put in his crop—or else he won't raise anything but kids!"

Ben ignored the teasing and went inside. There he hurriedly produced the license and held it out, trembling a little, waiting for the minister to wipe the steam from his spectacles.

"It appears to be in order, Deacon Barrett. Shall we proceed?"

Doshia followed the minister and Ben up the aisle to the front of the room, where she took a seat on the front bench with Philo and Hannah, who were keeping Charley quiet.

Stephen in his long black coat, with Ann on his arm, paused at the door until Julia Goodell began the march on her melodeon. Then as they stopped before the minister, he began to hurriedly intone the service as though to make up lost time. "Dearly beloved, we are gathered here in the sight of the Lord—"

What am I doing here? Ann thought in a flash—and tried to smile. She turned to look at the bearded, ungainly man beside her. Reverend Lorimer was demanding her attention: "Ann, do you take this man—"

Mechanically she made her responses. She shuddered inwardly at the phrase, "Til Death do you part."

At the final words, Ben stooped and kissed her. For one brief moment his eyes lost their shrewd piercing look, and he smiled down at her.

Charley, released, ran forward and grabbed Ann about her slender waist. She leaned down and swept him up in her arms.

"Now isn't that sweet!" Amelia Hanlon whispered to Debbie Hart.

"She will get her fill of that whippersnapper," Miss Debbie said pointedly as she reached to pick up her cloak and started up the aisle.

"Aren't you going up front to shake hands?" Amelia asked in astonishment.

"Young lady, I know when I'm not wanted. I came just to see the wedding finery. I've tried to warn her."

As Miss Debbie reached the rear of the room through the throng going forward, she gave Henry Laurie's coattail a jerk as she said in her rasping voice, "Let's get out of here!"

Chapter 12

Stanley, coming in from chores at breakfast time, sighted Ben in the kitchen and sang out lustily, "Well, I'm surprised to see you and sis up so early this morning—must be you didn't sleep well—or any."

Ben made no reply but turned away quickly and reentered the sitting room where Stephen was waiting. Ben was trying to be as casual as though he had spent the night on the floor upstairs, alone, as he had done once.

Meanwhile Ann was bustling around trying to help Doshia and Hannah with breakfast. Doshia was insisting for this time Ann should act like company. "Land sakes, child, you do look so—" then changed to, "My, I do hope Charley sleeps late. He was so tired! Did he bother you much in the night? You should have let me put him in our room like your father suggested."

"Oh no, he slept just fine."

Stephen's prayer and Bible reading lasted much longer than Ben remembered on the occasion two months before when the storm had detained him overnight. To add further to his discomfort, the Barretts sat a long time around the table, talking over the wedding.

Looking around her, Doshia said wearily, "This house is in such a mess—everything helter-skelter from the reception. You boys carry out the plank and nail kegs. I don't know how we would have seated forty people for refreshments without those benches against the wall."

"You and the girls did yourselves proud," Stephen said, looking across to Ben for approval, "serving creamed chicken and all that went with it to that crowd, and so quick after the ceremony."

"Your idea helped having the horse and buggy right there to bring Ann and Mr. Howe and me home. That was a short wedding trip for you folks."

Ben put down his coffee cup and wiped his whiskers with the back of his hand and looked at Ann sharply. "I think we had better finish our wedding trip this morning. I aim to move Ann and her things out home right away."

"But Mr. Howe," Doshia protested, "we had thought you two could stay here with us for several days. You could go back to the farm to tend your stock, and that would give Ann time to rest a little. She looks tired out—we've been so busy lately."

"Don't forget all the work I did, dressing old hens for creamed chicken. When Philo gets married, let's have something easier," Stan piped up.

"Don't worry, I'll not be marrying anyone in this town," Philo said tartly.

"You never can tell—look at Ann."

Doshia shook her head and frowned. Then, changing the subject, she said proudly, "Julia Goodell says our reception was every bit as nice as any she ever attended even back East."

"I liked it very much—all you did for us," Ben said solemnly. "But now it's over and I want to get through with the moving. I'll walk out home and get the oxen."

Doshia started to protest, but Ann shook her head and said simply, "Yes, of course, Mr. Howe."

It was nearly noon when Ben drove the oxen and cart up to the Barretts' front door. Doshia came out insisting, "It is practically dinnertime, Mr. Howe, and I can set on a pickup dinner in hardly no time—leftovers from the reception," she said and laughed.

"No, ma'am. I'm wanting to be loaded and on the way. We can eat out at the place."

Half an hour later, as Doshia came with an armload of Ann's clothes tied up in a sheet, Ben looked down from the cart and said, "I suppose you've got Charley's things somewhere in the load, Mrs. Barrett?"

"Oh, Mr. Howe, we planned to keep him until you folks get settled. The girls will take good care of him."

"Well, if you insist," Ben agreed readily.

Soon Ann came out, dressed in her long cloak and wearing her second-best bonnet, with her cashmere shawl drawn up about her shoulders. As she swept little Charley up in her arms, he reached to pull one of her long bonnet ribbons, and she put him down struggling. She went to the front of the cart and clambered up behind the cattle to perch herself on the very top of the load, on her new bureau. Ben climbed up stiffly beside her and without a word began testing the tie rope that secured the chairs that layed on top.

Ann turned to call down cheerily to her mother, "Don't look so sad! I'm not going far away, and I'll be back so often you won't even miss me."

Just as they were ready to start, Stephen came bringing his buffalo robe and tucked it carefully about her feet. As he stepped back, Ben slapped the nigh ox with the gee line, and the cattle, leaning into the yoke, started the cart moving.

Doshia stood at the front window crying silently, watching the couple atop the high, ungainly cart until they passed from sight beyond Hanlon's — thinking, on an ox cart — like she always said.

Facing the west wind that still bore the chill of winter. Ann did not try to talk much. It may have been the vibration of thet cart that made her voice tremble, so she tried keeping her muff to her face. Out on the prairie with the colony behind them, a dismal gray fog shut the cart within a world of its own in which they bounced along the grassy trail, over ground still half-frozen beneath the thick mat of dead grass. Red-winged blackbirds, bewildered by the cold, fluttered just ahead of the oxen, pausing, teetering on tall swaying stems of old grass. Overhead, crows cawing raucously wavered in a thin line across the dull sky, and a lone hawk circled and glided effortlessly.

"At this rate we'll make the two miles in less than an hour," Ben said, breaking the long silence. The cattle, hungry and thirsty, were ambling faithfully toward home.

"How soon can we see our house, Mr. Howe? I've never been out here except that one time — last fall."

"It's just a little ways now. You can see it from the top of the next rise. It's just a sod cabin, nowhere as nice as your father's house."

"But it will be our home, Mr. Howe."

They rode for some distance silently. Ben was watching her out of the corner of his eyes as she suppressed a yawn.

"I'm sorry, Mr. Howe. That wasn't polite of me. I didn't sleep much last night."

He made no reply.

She clutched at the course grimy sleeve of his work frock and turned to look up at him as she said timidly, "I'll try to be a better wife to you — next time."

He slapped the nigh ox with the gee line. "Well, I sure hope so. We're married now."

They bumped along in silence up another small hill.

"My land begins about here. I haven't broke out this side of my eighty yet. Guess you can't quite see the cabin—it's there on the second ridge."

As the cart started down toward the slough crossing, Ben pointed out the spring on the hillside below the squat log stable. "Good water, and only a hundred yards to carry to the cabin."

The cabin sitting low to the ground, blended into the dull grayness that was both sky and earth. A rusty stovepipe prodded its way through the sod-covered roof, shaggy with old grass. I didn't remember it this way, Ann thought. It was bright and sunny the day the baby was buried.

The oxen stopped to drink deeply from the trickle below the spring, then started briskly up the hill. As they passed the stable yard, the motley herd left off munching hay to peer through the rails at the oxen toiling past with their strange cargo. The cart circled the brow of the hill and stopped at the edge of the platform before the one door.

Ben climbed down stiffly. As he dropped the bows from the heavy yoke releasing the cattle, he looked up and said laconically, "Well, we got here."

Ann threw back the robe and slid down backward onto the tongue and to the ground. As Ben started toward the door he called back, "I'll get the fire started. It's way past my dinnertime!"

As she entered the kitchen, Ben was muttering the kindling was damp and wouldn't light. "Been shut up tight and no heat since yesterday. You'd better keep your wraps on till it warms up."

"My sakes, there's a lot of room in our cabin, Mr. Howe. It's really quite nice, and we will be real comfortable here."

"You can look around if you want to," he offered.

She crossed the kitchen and entered the tiny sitting room, teetering along on the boards that lay loose on the hard-packed dirt. A table, two straight-backed chairs, and a shelf tacked to the frame over which the sod had been laid composed its furnishings. This room and the small kitchen took up half of the cabin.

"I was never in a sod house before. I do believe it will be warmer than father's frame house."

"This gets damp in wet weather. Laura always complained—" he began.

"Which is our bedroom, Mr. Howe?"

"The one off from the kitchen."

Ann crowded past him as he bent over the bulky stove. Ben had tried to plaster over the sod walls with a thin coating of lime mixed with clay, but it was peeling badly and lay in rivulets along the edge.

"Oh, this will make a nice room for us, with my bedstead, the featherbed and my new bureau." She was trying desperately to sound cheerful.

As she stepped around the bed, a small black leather trunk protruding from beneath the high bed blocked her way. "What's in this trunk?" she called to him.

"Don't touch that trunk," he growled. "It's mine!"

Ann, rebuffed, stepped over the trunk and went to look out of the one window. There just inside the rail fence that enclosed the garden, two soggy mounds of fresh dug earth marked the graves of Laura and the baby. Old snow, dirty and shrunken, lay in patches in the lee of the fence. A path from the cabin led through the bars straight along the fence to the mounds.

A fire was burning merrily now. Ben stopped outside and returned saying, "Here's the stuff your mother insisted on sending. I'll be in for dinner soon as I throw down feed for the cattle."

Ann hastened to put some of the leftover chicken to heat, sliced some of Doshia's bread, and, rummaging, came up with a jar of wild plum butter.

When Ben entered, she was wearing a pretty white apron. She met him at the door and stretched on her tiptoes to plant a kiss on his cheek right above his whiskers. He looked surprised and puzzled.

"My, but you are tall, Mr. Howe," she said and laughed. "Can't you bend down just a little?"

He pushed her aside and went to remove his boots and work frock. Silently he dipped water from the bucket and began washing.

"This is almost like a picnic, isn't it, Mr. Howe," she said gaily as she passed the dish of chicken and biscuit. He enjoyed the food, taking a quantity of it, and eating fast. With forced cheerfulness she continued, "What do you think about clearing our room first so we can put the new furniture from home in there, Mr. Howe?"

He put down his coffee on the bare table and gazed at her in amazement. "What did you aim to do with the bed I've been using?"

"Well." She hesitated then said," I thought we could put that one in the other room—say, for company."

"Then what would you do with the one that's already there?"

She hesitated a moment, then answered boldly, "I didn't think it looked like much of a bed."

"What's wrong with it? I cobbled it up from crating boards," he said defensively.

"I just thought it would be nice to use the bedstead and the featherbed I brought. Then there's the bureau from father—that was almost our only wedding present—Oh, Mr. Howe, I'm so happy fixing up our room with my things."

He crossed the knife and fork on his plate and, shoving back from the table, said brusquely, "You've got a lot of stuff to stow away before bedtime. We'd better get the cart unloaded. For the life of me I can't see why you brought so much."

"But Mr. Howe, this is home now and I wanted to bring what I could—to help out."

"I suppose so, but Laura had a pretty good settin' out here."

Ann rose and silently began clearing the table, thinking, he speaks like she was really here.

As Ben started to do the evening chores, he pointed out the cave behind the cabin. "There's the potatoes there—and meat in the brine barrel in the lean-to. I'd like a decent supper. Our dinner wasn't much!"

"What about more water?" she asked.

"You know where the spring is—there where the oxen stopped. I'll bring you a bucket, if I think of it."

Darkness came early, pressing down about the lonely cabin, shutting out the dismal prairie. Indoors, the walnut shelf clock ticked away as if to break the silence, assisted by the cheerful crackling of the wood fire in the heating stove.

Later, Ann sat knitting beside the stove in her own rocker while Ben sat nodding in his straight-backed hickory chair opposite. At last she spoke, and the words sounded as though shouted in the stillness. "It's awful quiet, someway."

"What's that?" Ben asked, pretending to be wide awake.

"I guess it seems quiet because I miss having Charley running about—he is such a sweet child."

"Yes, that's right," he agreed mildly.°

Again Ben's head dropped lower and lower. Then, rousing himself, he got up and reached for one of the candles, saying sleepily, "It's time we went to bed."

"I've got to finish this one row across, Mr. Howe."

She put her candle on the new bureau and, taking her long flannel nightgown, dropped its ample folds over her head and began nervously fumbling herself out of her clothing. Only then did she turn toward the bed where Ben lay snuggled under two of her new comforters. As she knelt beside the bed, Ben raised up and said impatiently, "You'll get out of the habit here—floor is too cold and, besides, it's a waste of good time."

The candle cast weird shadows of Ben sitting up in bed throwing back the comforters for her.

Chapter 13

For two weeks following the wedding, spring delayed its arrival. Under Ann's capable hands the cabin became quite orderly and the indoor work an easy routine. Yet in the long days alone in the cabin she had too much time to think of her loneliness. However cheerfully she approached each day, her lightheartedness could not offset Ben's dour silences. His worry at each bad turn of the weather and his discouragement over their future baffled her. Once she lightly suggested Stephen's placid philosophy that seed time and harvest would never fail. Ben looked up from the endless stirring of his coffee and mumbled something about, "Your father isn't a poor settler, either."

Save for the first Sabbath after the wedding when they had attended meeting and stayed to dinner at the Barretts', Ann had neither seen nor had word from any of her family. Accustomed to living in a closely knit household, she missed the companionship — and especially missed Charley's childish prattle.

Two more Sabbaths passed, and each one found Ben reluctant to go to meeting. It was either too wet to walk to meeting or the oxen were loose on the prairie. Ann had anticipated with such pleasure her new role as hostess, offering tea and cookies to relatives and callers who came to tea. Yet none came.

Standing in the east window, she would look across the prairie to the scattered buildings of Goodell silhouetted against a pale morning sky. Or, of a late afternoon, she would watch the lowering sun glint upon their windows, hoping for sight of her father's buggy coming across the flat, coming out to tea.

Finally the warmth of coming spring, the drying ground, and her own need for work prompted her to announce at breakfast, "I think I'll clear off the garden today, and maybe you can get it plowed. I do want to have a good garden for you, Mr. Howe. Peas by the Fourth of July, as they say.

Ben looked up in mild amazement.

"I figured you'd come to your senses—about helping outdoors. Don't go settin' any fires—the prairie'd burn like tinder. And don't get so set on doing the garden you forget about dinner," he warned.

After the housework was done, Ann went to work armed with a wide wooden rake. From the very crest of the ridge she coudl see in all directions. Ben was sowing wheat on the fare end of the forty. His measured tread and rhythmical swinging arm were plainly visible as he strode back and forth with a seed pouch hung over his shoulder.

Across the wide valley to the south, swaying white-topped wagons moved slowly along the stage road. In the still air came faintly the rattle of trace chains, the creak of wagon wheels, and the shrill shouts of children herding small droves of cattle along the trail.

Ann carefully avoided glancing toward Goodell. I'm not going to look for them to come any more—then maybe they will—and bring Charley.

Turning to her task, she began raking the old dry cornsttalks, the brittle withered bean stems and pumpkin vines. On the far side of the garden she came upon a hoe whose rusty blade and gray weathered handle lay half buried beneath dead grass. Curious, she stooped to loosen it. This was Laura's. Slowly, almost reverently, she crossed the garden and carefully leaned the hoe against the rail fence beside the mound. She stood for a moment looking down at the tiny grave beside it, remembering vividly that crisp fall afternoon the baby was buried—and little Charley, how forlorn he had looked running wildly to catch Mr. Howe's hand as he returned toward the cabin from the graveside service. Here I am, she thought, taking up where Laura left off. If Mr. Howe would just be wanting to bring Charley home—so I can really begin to live!'

Ann tried to understand Ben's reluctance toward bringing the child home. Days crept into weeks and into a month and more since the wedding, and still he never spoke of bringing the boy home.

On the second Sabbath in May, by Ann's prearrangement, Emery drove out to the farm quite early, ". . . to see if you folks wouldn't like to go to meeting—and mother wants you to come to dinner too."

To save face, Ben accepted.

At dinner and again later, Stephen carefully repeated his growing concern over Doshia's weariness and her need of rest. This finally prompted Ben to say, "Ann and I want to take Charley home today. We are so lonesome for him."

Stephen and Doshia assented with just the right amount of reluctance.

As the buggy moved away, Charley squirmed around and called farewells, especially to Philo. She had been his first love. Then, sitting on "Aunt Ann's" lap, he faced the front, homeward-bound at last.

His days at the farm were happy ones — happy because they were full of adventure. In his childish imagination, the placid hens dusting themselves in the sawdust at the wood pile were wild game which scattered squawking nicely at his attack, armed with a stick gun. In fancy he spent hours riding the dooryard prairie mounted on the spread-legged sawbuck.

From the cabin Ann listened to the happy sounds of his play. This was the way she had wanted it to be — Charley nearby and safe. At the end of each adventurous day of play, she gathered him in to bathe in the wooden tub set on the kitchen floor.

"Why should I wash all over, Aunt Ann? Father doesn't — only once in a long time."

To this she would answer lightly, "Because I like a clean little boy the best."

"But wouldn't you love me if I was dirty?" he persisted.

The loneliness she had felt was over and past. The boy was constantly by her side as she went about her daily round of work in house and garden. Occasionally Ben took the child with him, but he was still in her thoughts. She felt a radiant pride in him.

Ben's interest in the child varied from day to day, according to his varying moods. Often the boy would shun his dour father and come running to Ann. She never failed to satisfy his wants.

After one of his father's sharp rebukes, she saw the child circle the cabin and follow the worn path to the garden. She watched him fumble the thong on the gate and entering, go directly to Laura's grave. For a whole minute he stood looking down; then, raising his head, stood motionless looking out across the prairie to the west. Minutes later she watched him steal away, but he did not come near her. For the first time she realized that to the child she was only a stepmother after all.

It was midmorning in early summer when Stephen Barrett drove his horse and buggy up the hill toward the cabin. Charley darted across the door yard to meet him, and Stephen stopped to help him clamber up.

The boy babbled excitedly, "We thought you were never coming after us, and Aunt Ann wants to see the band and everything."

"But Charley, you want to see the Fourth of July parade, too?"

"I don't know—I never went before."

"Your grandma and I thought it would be nice to have you folks come to dinner, and then you could see for yourself what goes on."

"Papa don't want to go," the child said bluntly.

"Oh, that's too bad. We wanted all our family together today."

"He says it's a waste of time."

The child's shrill voice evidently carried to the cabin, for Ben followed Ann out of the door, slamming it behind.

"I kept telling Ann it will be too crowded," Ben protested, "but she insisted."

"Why, there's lots of room," Stephen assured him, "with you holding Ann on your lap and Charley helping me drive."

Halfway across the flat Charley piped up, "I can hear the church bell. Do we have to go to meeting before the parade?"

Stephen laughed. "Well, son, it's the same bell, only today it isn't calling us to meeting." He chuckled. "It's been jangling that way since before sun-up."

"Is Mr. Forbes ringing it like he does for the Sabbath?"

"No, Charley. Some boys are ringing it."

"Uncle Stan?"

"No, or at least I hope not. It sure woke up the town early."

"What are they going to have besides the parade?" Ben asked, displaying interest in the affair now he was on his way.

"Of course there will be the reading of the Declaration of Independence—it wouldn't be the Fourth without that. Then they have asked our new lawyer, Sam Cook, to make a patriotic speech."

"He is quite a pusher, that Cook," Ben said. "I haven't had any time for him since he defended that horse thief last spring!"

"Oh, I wouldn't feel that way," Stephen said mildly. "The accused must be defended even for horse stealing."

As the buggy pulled up at the kitchen door, Charley hopped down calling for "Aunt Philo." But Philo and Stan and most of the other people of the colony had already assembled at Goodell's park, where the parade was forming.

At Charley's begging, his father and Stephen sauntered down the road with him to meet the parade. In the lead came a pompous little man carrying the flag, strutting along over the ruts in the road.

"Didn't I tell you Sam Cook was a pusher? Look at him make like he was a soldier," Ben sniffed in disgust.

Behind the flag bearer; almost nosing his coattails, plodded the lead pair of Andy Sheridan's four yoke of oxen pulling a big freighter. Andy kept yanking on the gee line and calling, "Whoa up," to slow the cattle to Sam's measured tread. The big wagon was fairly bursting with boys hooking a ride, envied by those too young, and the girls. Behind the freighter marched the brass band spread out widely to make a good showing as they played the "Star Spangled Banner." Next came a squadron of local boys on horseback. A few had real saddles.

When the parade had passed, Stephen said, "Let's go home and see if Charley's grandma has dinner ready. You didn't want to hear the speech, did you?"

"I'd just as soon hear the Declaration read again, but not Cook's speech!"

As they approached the house, Ben said, "Your place looks real nice painted white, even with the fence, Deacon."

"We miss the old home back east," Stephen confided, "so likely that's why we fixed this one up as near like it as we could. He chuckled. "The fence, though isn't just for looks. It's to keep the town hogs from running under the house and scratching their backs. They used to shake the whole place."

"I aimed to fix up my cabin before another winter, but now I can't see my way clear—losing Laura and all. I tell you, Deacon, it's pretty hard for a man to make a living for a family on eighty acres and get ahead any. If I just had more land close by."

As they entered the kitchen, Doshia turned from the stove and greeted Ben as Mr. Howe. Someway he appeared so old and serious that a first name sounded too familiar—even if he was Ann's husband.

When they were seated at the long table in the kitchen, Stephen looked around in surprise. "I declare I never noticed Philo and Stan aren't here. I suppose is is that Peck boy again." Turning to Ann and Ben, he said lightly. "This John Peck just came out from Maine a while back. He works at Clack's flour mill. I guess he must have seen Philo somewhere. Anyway, I nearly stepped on him in the dark sitting on our kitchen steps getting up the courage to knock."

"But Philo," Ann murmured in amazement.

"Yes, and she hasn't mentioned going back East since."

The meal was half over when Philo and then Stan slipped into their places. Stephen teased them and, except Ben, everyone joined in the laughter.

After a bit Ben said in rather an accusing tone, "I hear there was a runaway slave in town last week and old Cap Clack was hiding him at the mill. First thing we know there'll be trouble about it in this town. Old Clack and the ones that passes them on toward Canada will be to blame," Ben concluded heatedly.

"It could be," Stephen said with quiet unconcern.

Finding himself the center of attention, Ben continued, "Don't none of us have any business meddlin' in this slavery fight. I don't aim to take sides. The way I see it, they're property same as oxen or anything."

There was a long silence while the family seemed to be very busy eating. Stephen was thinking there was no use in getting heated up over this thing—after all, he was Ann's husband.

Stanley looked up from his plate and, catching Philo's attention, winked slyly.

Chapter 14

Snow came early that winter of 1856-57. Still busy husking corn from the shocks in the field behind the stable, Ben had paid little attention to the wood pile until snow came. Immediately he began worrying about firewood and inquired for a man to work for board and washing.

In early December, Andy Halden arrived afoot from out west, with his worldly possessions crammed in a gunnysack. He was a shifty, water-eyed little man with a scraggly sandy-colored beard. At first sight of him Ann whispered, "He looks like a drinking man!"

"Possible," Ben said laconically, "but I figure he can help me get up some wood and besides that, I've another idea we'll work on," he added mysteriously. "You don't need to be scared of him—like if you was here alone with him—he is too old to be dangerous—must be fifty."

"I wish you didn't have to away so much, Mr. Howe."

"I'll tend to planning the work and hire who I like. It won't cost much to feed him, after we do the butchering."

At supper Ann tried to make the stranger welcome, though she felt skeptical about him. She tried to ask about his family and where he had been recently. Andy Halden kept his own counsel. He might have been in the Colorado gold rush, but he could tell nothing convincing about it.

At breakfast the following Sabbath, Ben asked, "Who is going with me to meeting?" Andy looked up from his eating, knife in hand, "I got to throw down more hay to the cattle." He drank deeply from his saucer, confident he had avoided meeting.

"You two men go," Ann suggested helpfully. "It's too cold for Charley and me to ride in the ox cart."

The Reverand Lorimer could be depended on to dwell on the evil of drink sometime during his hour-and-a-half sermon, and Ben felt it his duty to expose Andy to some religion.

When they returned from meeting, Ben brought word that Doshia was sick in bed, and had been for some days. About all Dr. Holt had done was to draw a little blood from her every other day.

"I do wish I'd known it," Ann said anxiously. "I'd have even walked to town with you, so I could do for her — Philo is so helpless."

"You couldn't have done much in such a short time. You have to remember you have a family to look after, yourself."

Ann looked up from the stove, baffled by his indifference. He could not know she had been counting the days since she had been away from the cabin.

Those December days dragged slowly. Shut away from all contact with her own family by the weather and Ben's insistence that someone else could do for her mother, Ann bided her time.

At breakfast the day before Christmas, Ben announced, "Andy and me are going to the timber again, soon's the sun is up. We got to have more wood. You get our lunch right away—you can eat later."

"It don't seem like you've brought home much wood lately, considering the days and days you've spent in the timber."

"We've been busy every day, haven't we, Andy?"

"You damn tootin', and we're tuckered out come night, ma'am. You'd ought to see the pile we've got there."

Ben glanced at Andy and shook his head, then quickly offered, "Pretty cold again last night—thickest crust on the snow I ever remember."

"You mean it would hold me up?" Ann asked anxiously.

"It might, but don't go trying it. And mind you, don't let Charley outside he might freeze or something."

Ann stood in the window watching when the men were ready to start. A pale sun was just rising beneath a low bank of frosty clouds that appeared to rest on the Goodell ridge. The men circled the cabin, walking beside the oxen to keep warm, and struck out along the ridge toward the timber near the Sugar Creek crossing. The men strode along on the crust while the oxen dragging the heavy sled swayed and wavered, reluctant to push through the drifts breast deep. Their warm breath rose in little cloudlike puffs. Behind them, jagged crust lay scattered like the rough wake of a boat in quiet water.

By midmorning the sun had all but disappeared behind slate-gray clouds and gave no warmth. Ann almost gave up her idea of walking home, aghast at her own boldness in rebelling against Ben's strict order. Then, as suddenly, she decided to go.

Charley was jubilant at the prospect of "a nice walk to see grandma." Cooped up in the cabin for days, he shouted for joy as she dressed him for the trip. As she stepped outside, she noted the wind was rising. Taking Charley's mittened hand, they started. Beyond the scant protection of the stable and the haystacks, the cold penetrated all the layers of their clothing. But she was determined to walk to town.

Up on the flat the wind struck them with full force. The first half-mile left Ann exhausted and dazed. Hanlon's farmhouse two miles away at the edge of town never seemed to get closer. Every few steps the crusted snow gave way, plunging her knee-deep in soft snow, from which she must climb to resume walking. Charley, striding manfully on the crust, would pause to pull her up. For a time he endured it better than Ann.

Breathless, her back to the wind, she stopped to rest and examine the child for frostbite. In that brief moment he turned toward the wind and, gasping for breath in the cold, began whimpering piteously. Then it began to snow, small hard-frozen flakes that stung as the wind blasted them against the two.

She was dizzy from the buffeting of the wind and numbed by cold, yet she caught a glimpse of some house in th distance. Dully she thought "Is that Hanlons—or is it Harrisons back on the prairie? I've got to know." Even as she hesitated the dim outline faded. Moments later it appeared in another direction.

Frantically she pulled off a mitten to wipe the snow that clung frozen to her eyelashes. But the cold numbed her fingers before she could clear it away. When she tried to look again, the one landmark had vanished in the mad, whirling storm.

Charley quit his whimpering and stood humped over, pulling down heavily. As she leaned down he slumped drowsily to the snow. Franctically she pulled him up, slapped him sharply, and yelled in his ear, "Let's dance—here—like this!" She began lifting him up and dropping him onto the crust as she moved her feet faster and faster. Her long skirts billowing in the wind gave some protection to the child huddled against her. Ripping off her mittens, she warmed his face until the cold was unbearable. She resumed the dancing, but the child showed no interest. Then she made her decision. With heads bent low, they turned and began struggling toward where home must surely be. The wind had leveled over all trace of their own footprints. She stumbled, rested, and stumbled again.

Haunted by fear she was leading the child in endless circles, desperately she fought off the stupor of exhaustion. She had no fear of death for herself. It would be so easy to drop into the snow once she had given Charley over to Mr. Howe. The roar of the storm might well be celestial music to which she was doomed to march, eternally dragging the child back to find his father.

Franctically she beat her arms and slapped her snow-encrusted face. The sting renewed her determination. Later, she dully imagined Ben was calling her from somewhere behind the impenetrable curtain of snow. She heard his booming voice, and, when a shadow flitted past, she turned square about and struck a slender object waist high above the snow. With one hand she clung to it for a full minute before recognizing it was a surveyor's stake — a section corner.

Bending over, she brushed at the snow that encrusted the rough bark. It was a bit of hickory sapling. Vaguely she remembered a hickory stake — Charley had asked if it would grow to be a tree — but it was the corner of Mr. Howe's land — or was it at Harrisons over on the other road? Again she stopped to listen, and once more in the roar of the storm she thought Ben was calling for Charley. Summoning her last bit of courage, she grasped the child's hand and, leaving the stake, staggered toward the voice. After scarce a dozen steps she came upon ground where the snow lay shallow, and she no longer broke through the crust. Then as hope faded she came onto a clump of swamp grass around which the snow had eddied and left bare. She had found the slough below the stable. Through the storm its dim outline appeared. In the lee of the stable she paused again to warm the child's bare face; then, slapping him sharply on the rump, dragged him staggering the last few yards to the cabin.

Safely inside, she called out weakly for Ben, then dully realized he was miles away at the timber. Replenishing the fire, she set about unwrapping the drowsy child, fumbling feverishly with the knots of the frozen muffler, thinking — Mr. Howe will never forgive me if I've let him freeze.

Alternately she feared Ben's return with his certain wrath — and the next moment feared lest he perish in the storm. Later, she decided to tell him herself of her attempt to get to town, for then he would know how badly she wanted to get away from this cabin—and to go see about her mother.

An hour or so later, as she sat with the child drowsy in her lap, she straightened up suddenly and asked brightly, "Do you know tomorrow is Christmas?"

The child showed slight interest.

"We must think of something to give your father for a Christmas present when he comes home. What do you think he'd like?"

"Mince pies," he said emphatically.

"That would be nice because he likes them," she conceded, vaguely thinking of the pies as a peace offering also.

"But what will there be for you, Aunt Ann?"

"Let's see," she began, pretending deep thought.

"You have to tell," he commanded.

"No one but you can give me what I want the very most."

"What's that?"

"That you always call me 'mother.' That would be the nicest present in the whole world for me."

The child's face clouded. "But you aren't my mother—you're Aunt Ann."

Outside the storm raged unabated as the hours dragged slowly past. For herself she had little to fear within the thick sod walls and with wood in the lean-to-beside the door. She tried not to let Charley know her worry over Ben.

After the supper dishes were washed, she gathered the child up in her lap and told him the old, old story of the Star the Wise Men followed to find the Babe in the Manger.

"Can we see the Star tonight?" he asked with awe. "I hope he sends a Star to bring papa and Mr. Halden home."

"We will pray that He will keep them safe till tomorrow."

Ann rose early the next morning, restless in her concern for Ben. With the child still asleep, she stood a long time at the frost-encrusted window watching the sun rise over the Goodell ridge. The distant buildings looked like tiny dots adrift on a vast sea of white. Bitterly she thought, "It's thirty-one days since I've been away from this—place. I did so want to be with the folks for Christmas."

At midmorning Ben arrived with half a sledload of wood, and in the excitement of his return Ann forgot her resolve to tell him everything. Perhaps it was better that he got the disconnected story from Charley, as he held the boy on his lap while warming his feet at the cookstove.

"And then we made mince pies for your present." The secret finally came out.

Something seemed to stir a long suppressed emotion in Ben, for he drew the child closer and planted a tickling kiss down his neck, laughing heartily all the while, Ann, half-expecting to share in this rare burst of affection, kept busy nearby.

Charley was concluding with, "I think it was going to be Christmas at Grandpa's, too, but Aunt Ann—I mean Mother and me, we couldn't get there. We had to come home and make pies for you, Papa."

"Where did you men stay?" Ann asked hurriedly.

"At old Bob Rose's cabin."

"How is Maria? I never get to see her any more."

"Old Bob is talking of going west. Says it's gettin' too crowded around here—settled up too thick."

After a time, Ben said to Andy, "Soon as you throw off that jag of wood, I think we'll butcher the hog—good a day as any,"

Listening, Ann thought bitterly, butchering on Christmas Day! I should be used to such. He plans to keep me busy making the lard and cooking sausage so I won't mind being shut up here in this—place.

Chapter 15

It was September of '58 when Ann first suspected she would bear Ben a child in the spring. When there was no longer any doubt, she still felt no elation. Her fear of the ordeal was heightened by old wives' tales of first babies born only after days of struggle and pain. Vaguely she wondered if in the meantime she would lose what little affection Ben bore her.

When Doshia noticed her thickening figure she said quite calmly, "So I am to have a grandchild at last. I suppose Ben is pretty happy about it."

Ann hung her head as she murmured, "If he is, he never said so. He is pretty gruff about it mornings when I'm just too sick to let him—"

"I know, child," Doshia said gently, "it is always that way, I guess."

If Doshia Barrett had any pride at the prospect of a first grandchild, it did not prompt her to offer any help in preparation for the event. The Barretts had been cautious of offering the young couple any material help. Ben was known to be sensitive at his own failure to provide any but the bare necessities for his family. That very summer he had been compelled by the rapid deterioration of the sod cabin, to strip the sod from the frame and rebuild it into a small but comfortable house. He had broken prairie day after day for two dollars an acre in exchange for the carpenter work; and much of the lumber came from the saw logs he and Andy had cut as a surprise to Ann. In fact, the rebuilding of the house had all been a surprise.

For Ann time began passing relentless fast. There was so much to do and so little time to do it all. Ben was away at work so much that fall, leaving to her the task of digging the beets and turnips and onions and storing them in dry dirt in the new cellar. Alone all day after Charley now seven and in his first term at school, left at sunrise to ride with Ben, she worked doggedly at the heavy task.

On days when the boy was home he was of little help to her. She tried all manner of games and goals to encourage him—counting turnips into the bucket or searching for the largest beet. But Charley hated to get his hands dirty and invented excuses to leave the garden. Stalling for time, he would saunter back eventually with the maddening slowness of a child. No inducement could hurry the stolid slowness of the child, nor keep him at work.

A touch of frost in mid-October turned brown the leaves of Ben's cane patch beyond the stable. At once he gave up all other work and began to cut and haul the giant stalks to Baird's mill at the edge of the townsite. There a patient horse circled endlessly at the end of a long pole, turning the rollers, crushing the stalks and sending sweet watery juice gushing into wooden barrels.

Back home again, Ben hurried to set up the big shallow syrup pans on flat stones in the door yard. As he started toward the wood pile he called over his shoulder to Ann, "We better get a batch to boiling right away—warm as it is the stuff might spoil. Once we get our molasses we won't have to pay Shute for any more high-priced sugar!"

Half an hour later, Deacon Forbes drove into the yard with his new team and wagon, and called to Ben who was still filling the pans, "Heard at the mill you were boiling syrup today, so I brought Francis over to help. He isn't doing a thing around home."

Even as his father was speaking, the boy jumped out and began stirring the juice with the long paddle. Ann came out of the kitchen wearing one of Ben's old work frocks and with a red bandana handkerchief tied about her head. She waved, but did not come closer.

"Looks like your foot must have slipped, Ben, the deacon said, nodding in her direction. "I see you're expecting an increase in the family, come spring."

"Could be," Ben replied evasively.

Will strolled slowly to the stable and stood leaning on the rail fence. Ben followed reluctantly, wondering what was coming next.

"Ann is getting along in years, and this first birth may go hard with her. Take an old man's advice, Ben, and don't let her do lifting and carrying heavy loads—nor walking a great lot when it's slippery come winter."

"It's hard to keep her from overdoing," Ben said defensively. "Nowlike this syrup boiling today—she is aiming to do a lot of that, though I keep telling her she shouldn't," Ben lied glibly.

Will continued, "Lydia says to tell you we just as well take you folks to meeting—not over a mile out of our way. And that's nothing, now I've got me a team," he added with pride.

So that's how it is, Ben thought after Deacon Forbes had gone, the neighbors figuring I ain't careful about Ann. I'll take her to meeting myself—with the oxen—twon't be long she will be too fat to be seen in public anyway.

So, for several weeks Ben yoked the oxen to the cart and took Ann and Charley to meeting. At Stephen's hearty urging they began taking Sabbath dinner at the Barretts. Emery and Hannah would come from their new house down by the mill—more glad than anyone knew to get a substantial meal.

At these family dinners Stan and Philo were always teasing. After a preliminary skirmish Stan would invariably say, "Philo is waiting for John Peck to grow up or make up his mind."

Once Ann came to Philo's rescue with, "Take your time picking out a husband, sis."

"Gee, she is practically an old maid now," Stan exploded, "and she has been making eyes at John for three years."

With that, Stan ducked toward the sitting room where his father was visiting with Ben. Stephen tried to talk of matters Ben would find interesting. This time they were talking of the new-fangled threshing machine that might do away with flailing grain by hand. That had lead up to the importance of livestock in prairie farming. As Stan entered the room, Ben was saying, with an unusual note of confidence in his voice, "I figure there'll be a better market for pork and for wheat, too, when the railroad builds closer to us."

Emery, who had been listening, shook his head.

"I was at Iowa City a few days ago, and the track ends along there in the Amana Colony. Likely they have run out of money again."

"That's odd," Ben said as his face clouded, "I heard over at George Chapin's tavern they were going to start grading toward the east from here come spring." Disgruntled, he continued, "I wanted to work a yoke of cattle on the grading job, but with Ann in her shape and not able to help any this spring —"

There was a silence until Stephen spoke. "This slavery business looks bad, Ben. I declare Buchanan and that weak-minded Supreme Court are going to ruin the country allowing the curse to spread into new states out west. I tell you, Ben, this country can't go on forever being part free and part slave."

Ben snorted, "This town will be in trouble and maybe see blood shed if folks don't quit meddlin' with slaves — the underground — bah! It riles me to think of such foolishness — hauling black people around in buggies at night — toward Canada."

"We all have our ideas about it," Stephen said mildly. "We can't settle it — and besides, Doshia is calling dinner."

From the head of the long table in the kitchen, in a silence broken only by the clock on the wall, Stephen talked with unusual earnestness to his God. He ended with, "and bring us peace and most of all please give us understanding of one another."

At breakfast the following Sabbath, Ben calmly announced the weather looked too bad for going to meeting.

"It does look threatening," she said in level tones.

"You are showing too much to be seen in public," he said firmly, eyeing her critically. "Folks will begin to talk. Seems like all your dresses make you look big as a barrel."

Ann got up quickly and began clearing the table. Bitter resentment boiled within her.

It was evening before she mustered courage to ask shyly with a forced laugh, "Wives don't cost an awful lot do they Mr. Howe?"

No answer.

"I'll venture you'd never guess how little I've spent on myself since I was married."

Ben put down the old Iowa City paper he was reading and stared at her in amazement.

"I've only had one cheap little lawn dress and two changes of bonnet ribbon," she announced proudly.

"You mean to say you've worn out all those dresses you brought when you came out here to live?"

"Well — no, they are not quite worn out yet, but I thought I'd like something new for a change — maybe a plain wool dress made so I wouldn't show so much."

"You won't be going out much till warm weather anyway."

Ann got up quickly and went to the kitchen to busy herself at nothing. Through the door she could see Ben sitting bolt upright in his chair staring straight ahead. A few minutes later he got up and shuffled past her into the bedroom. She heard the black leather trunk slide from under the bed. Dejectedly Ann thought—he is brooding over Laura again.

Later, the lid slammed and Ben appeared in the doorway saying in level tones, that were part irritation and part condescension, "Here is a right good worsted dress that was Laura's. She never did get to wear it much—and Philo could help fit it."

If he had suddenly struck her, Ann could not have been more surprised than at the proffer of dress from the trunk. Quickly she realized it would be that dress or none. Later she thought—he does care about me—to give me a dress that was Laura's. Now she knew better than to ask for money to buy cloth for little garments she would soon need.

March weather turned bad, with cold drizzling rain, then snow squalls and high winds. To Ann, misshappen, awkward, and discouraged, only the certain coming of spring kept her from despair. A fitful wind blew wet snow across the garden that had been bare and muddy the day before. Now it was bleak and chill with no promise of spring. Standing at the bedroom window, Ann looked across to the two graves with their weathered rough-sawn boards, wondering if he would bury her beside them. For her there was no beauty in the familiar scene that day. Each new flurry of snow was holding back the time that would bring her release.

As she turned disconsolately from the window, she caught sight of Ben's old leather trunk and remembered how he had barked at her for even looking at it, that very first day at the cabin. Bending with difficulty, she hauled it forth and struggled with the stiff leather straps. Cautiously she raised the lid. Under a fading copy of the Springfield, Massachusetts, *Gazette* of November, 1854, lay carefully folded a wine-colored merino dress. "It must have been her wedding dress," Ann whispered reverently, as she laid it on the bed.

Tucked in the folds of a wool petticoat lay a small carved picture case in which two dim photographs faced each other. One was of a serious, whiskered young man—the other of a smiling, pink-cheeked woman.

Hurrying, Ann dug deeper seeking the tiny garments she needed so badly. There on the bottom, sure enough, lay the sturdy hand-woven things she sought—tiny gowns that seemed doll size—little shirts and bands of fine wool and knitted stockings.

She closed the lid and, rising with difficulty, gathered the tiny garments in her arms. Outside the sun burst through the clouds and shone brightly. Ann Howe was more cheerful than she had been for many a day.

Chapter 16

At breakfast in mid-April, Ann calmly reminded Ben that was the day she was going to Emery and Hannah's for her confinement. Ben stopped his hurried eating and looked at her sharply.

"Well, if you think you should, go right ahead! For the life of me I don't see why you wouldn't be as well off having it at home the way other women do. I planned to run to town and get Doc Holt when you really needed him."

As he was speaking, through Ann's mind ran the memory of Ben running to get Tom Holt the day Laura's baby died. Despite that thought, she spoke cheerfully now. "There's a pot of beans on the back of the stove, and steamed bread in the pantry. I baked white bread yesterday—four loaves."

"That'll help a little," he said grudgingly. "Likely you'll be home again in a week, won't you?"

"I don't know, Mr. Howe, I'll try to be."

Sitting at the table, fearful and dejected, she looked up as he arose, expecting some sign of encouragement or affection from him. Instead, he took down his work frock and hat ready to go to the field.

"Mr. Howe," she began in a low tone, almost pleadingly, "if anything happens—my folks will take care of the children."

Ben pulled open the door and left without replying.

Three hours later, Philo came driving Stephen's horse and buggy and entered the kitchen cheerily. "Lovely morning for a ride, sister. From the looks of your carpetbag, you're planning to go east— east to town, that is."

A quick smile lighted Ann's face. *She is being cheerful just to keep up my courage,* she thought.

While Philo waited, Ann moved slowly about the house, seeing it critically, smoothing a wrinkle in a bedspread here, or straightening a rag rug there. She did not feel ready to leave even as she followed Philo to the buggy. She stood slowly scanning the prairie as if to fix it in her mind. A warm April sun had set the heat waves to shimmering above the fresh-turned earth where Ben was plowing on the back forty.

"We are in no hurry, sister," Philo said, "because I like also to stop once in a while and listen to the world around me."

Somewhere in the distance mourning doves repeated their five-note melancholy call. "Let's go," Philo said, Picking up her reins. "Those plaguy things make me sad just hearing them."

As they topped the rise beyond the slough, Ann turned a little to look back at the farmhouse on the ridge. Philo sensed her thoughts and said, "It's changed a lot in three years, sis."

"It will be different when I come back," Ann said slowly and turned her face toward town.

Comfortably and cheerfully settled at Emery and Hannah's, Ann waited for her time. After only one night there she remarked gratefully, "My, it's good to rest and such fun to laugh again."

"If I had that old sober sides for a husband," Hannah sputtered, "I'd tickle his ribs or something—to make him laugh. I don't think Ben gets anything out of life but work!"

"He is awfully busy, especially now," Ann apologized. "Likely he was too late with his chores to come in afoot last night." To this Hannah replied reassuringly, "Probably he will be in tonight."

But Ben did not come that evening or the next.

Charley, in school two blocks away, came at least once a day— "to see Aunt Ann—how she feels." On entering, he would look around carefully for signs of the new baby.

The boy was apparently having a wonderful time at the Barretts being showered with attention. He had other items to report. Once he had gone with Stephen to watch the gang grading for the railroad. Again he related his good fortune, announcing proudly, "My Aunt Philo is making me a pair of pants, and she is making them longer in the legs than these—they come way down below my knees. I'm growing up, and my pants have to be longer, she says."

"You are my big boy," Ann said proudly. "I know you needed the pants."

"But Grandpa didn't like for me to have new pants," he piped shrilly, "because Aunt Philo cut up a pair of his."

"We always do that," Ann assured him.

"There isn't anything left of them now! She is cutting pieces for quilts out of the scraps. I think she is going to get married to John Peck. She asked him how he'd like a nice warm quilt to sleep under."

Four days later Ann gave birth to a baby girl with pale blue eyes and a trace of light brown hair. The capable Hannah and Dr. Holt assisted in the long ordeal.

Hours later, as Ann lay recovering consciousness, she rolled her head wearily from side to side as though searching for someone among those by her bedside. Then she closed her eyes and drifted off again.

Stan went horseback to tell Ben the good news. Later, he reported in low tones to Hannah in the kitchen, "He took it real calm even when I told him it was a girl. Don't tell sis, but I thought he was mighty indifferent about it. He acted like he was itching to go on plowing, so I left."

It was the next Sabbath, and after meeting at that, when Ben knocked at Emery's door. Hannah greeted him with more warmth than she felt he deserved, then stood listening at the foot of the stairs, hoping for Ann's sake he would show some concern for her and the baby. From the casual tone of his voice he seemed to be displaying very mild interest in either. After scarcely five minutes Hannah heard Ben's restless footsteps move toward the door. As she left her listening post she heard Ann say insistently, "Come over here, Mr. Howe, so you can really see your little Alice."

The pacing stopped.

"Is that what you've been calling it?"

"Why yes, Mr. Howe, I thought it was a pretty name."

"Put 'Laura' in there — I'm not forgetting her. You might know I'd want to name it. We'll call her Alice Laura."

Ann's assent was lost to Hannah in the clatter of Ben's boots on the stairs. At the right time she reappeared out of the kitchen and asked innocently, "Isn't she a sweet baby? My land, Emery and I envy you that beautiful little girl."

"She's all right," Ben replied in an indifferent tone.

"Won't you stay for dinner?" Emery asked jovially.

"No, I am going over to your father's for dinner and to see my boy."

There was a ring of pride in the last two words.

Ann and her baby stayed at Emery's ten days, then moved across to Stephen's. He hired a German emigrant girl to help Doshia and later to go with Ann back to the farm.

During all this time Charley received particular attention from callers who came to see the new baby. He thrived on it. For a time it was nice being the big brother to such a cute little sister as they all said she was. And during those days, Ann did seem to pay heed to him besides doting a lot over the baby. This eased his feelings.

Back again at the farm Charley began to notice his mother did not want to go with him on expeditions as she had done the previous summers. The first school day after their return from Stephen's, he begged her to go with him part way across the flat toward school, as she had once done. Perhaps unconsciously he was testing her to see if she cared as much for him as before the coming of the new baby.

It was some time later that Miss Lucy Bigsby remarked at meeting about Charley's poor school attendance. Yet the boy had left home each morning with his lunch pail and always returned at the usual time, tired and hungry. It remained a mystery until Ben found bits of breadcrust wrapped in a piece of Iowa City newspaper beside a small dam in the brook downstream out of sight from the farmhouse.

When Ben reported this to Ann, he appeared amused by the boy's cleverness and declared the term was about over anyway. To this Ann replied that she hoped he would get some help out of the boy, as the child was no earthly help to her when she needed just a little. Ben made the same biting comment he used frequently, "You're not the hand with him that Laura was!" This time he concluded with, "The boy likes to roam around and be independent. Now don't go tying him to your apron string."

The first serious trouble started at dinnertime in late August. Ann was busy getting dinner on the table and talking to his father about a trip to town, and didn't pay a bit of attention to Charley's account of the ground squirrel he had almost snared that very morning. To make matters worse, the baby cried and his father actually offered to hold the little mite, and sat dandling it on his knee. Charley slipped away from the table and retreated to his wickiup back in the corn field. A little later the soft rustling of the leaves may have drowned out his father's lusty calls. Stubbornly the boy continued whittling arrows from a bunch of willow twigs. After a bit he heard the squeal of the ox cart going toward town — and they had not begged him to go.

Charley never really intended to go far nor stay long, when he circled the house and started the trail toward Sugar Creek carrying his bow and new arrows. A faint haze telling of distant grass fires pleased his nostrils. There was no one to call him back. Somewhere in the timber that bordered the creek, the strident song of the locust lured him.

He waded at the ford for a while, then started to go downstream—"Just a little ways," he promised himself, muttering. Two hours later he came out of the timber three miles down, at Bob and Rose's cabin.

At noon the next day, after catching a ride part way, the boy stealthily approached home. To his disappointment his father and Ann were eating dinner quite calmly, and she hadn't even put his plate on the table.

Ben said very little to the wanderer. Ann felt greater relief than she cared to show. She felt it was all her fault and had said so. Ben said nothing to dissuade her. Somehow she had failed the boy. Despite her efforts to make him feel loved and wanted, he had grown away from her. Some inborn wanderlust outweighed her respect for Ann and his home.

Chapter 17

At midmorning of Thanksgiving Day of 1860, Ann drove up to Stephen's door with little Alice propped up on the seat of the rickety buckboard next to Charley. In vain she had tried to induce Ben to come to dinner, finally adding "I think Philo and John are going to be married tonight—and you'd want to be there, wouldn't you, Mr. Howe?"

Ben was determined not to go. He made excuses—too much to do before winter—husking corn from the shocks—and besides, it looked like a storm.

So she had driven away, thankful that he was at least speaking. His days of bitter silence hurt deeply.

As she drove across the prairie flat toward town, she was almost more thankful for the new horse than for most any other blessing. She still marveled at Ben spending all of a hundred dollars' gold for Nellie. At the time, she had felt the horse was a peace offering he had brought her following three days during which he had not spoken a word to her.

At home again next day, at dinner she gave a lively account of all that had happened, hoping to make Ben feel he belonged to the family. It was easier having something to talk about when he was getting over a stubborn silent streak.

"Philo only got two wedding presents—old Mrs. Southlin gave her a silver teaspoon—and father gave her that forty acres east of the townsite—the land he bought off Lol Phipps that first year."

Ben's eyes opened.

"You say he gave her forty acres?" he asked incredulously.

"Why yes," she said and laughed. "He used to say he bought it just for that, though none of us thought Philo would ever stay in Goodell, much less marry anyone here."

"John's been a long time making up his mind," Ben said dryly. "I wonder what decided him—the forty acres or did they have to get married?"

"I really think it was account of the war talk, ever since Lincoln was elected," Ann rattled on. "Philo says John would volunteer if there is a war, so they want to enjoy living together while they can. Our folks are settin' them up to housekeeping in a cute little house down there opposite the mill where John works."

"You mean they got all that besides the forty acres?"

"Yes. Why not?"

"Well, if John volunteers I say he's crazier than I thought," Ben said, turning away in disgust.

"It does seem awful, all this war talk, and right here in our own country," she said thoughtfully. "Why, you might even have to go, Mr. Howe, or Charley, if it lasts as long as some think."

Ben smiled rather smugly and said, "I'm too old, and my boy is way too young. If you'd worry less and work more you'd be better off."

Charley, listening, grinned with satisfaction.

"What did you do all afternoon, Ben inquired searchingly, "just sit and think."

"We womenfolk mostly just sat and listened. Sam Cook and his wife were there—John had him get the license when he was at the county seat, so Father thought they should be invited. Mrs. Cook is so nice."

"That's more than anybody but a horse thief could say about Sam!"

Ann ignored that remark.

Father asked Mr. Cook if he thought there'd be war. Sam was captain in the Mexican War, remember?"

"I'm sure he said there would be one. I suppose he is itching to get to fighting again. It would be one way to get him out of town!"

"Reverend Heath said we should let the South have their slaves. He said we must be patient, and he even said we should let those states leave the Union if they want."

"I'll bet Sam Cook wouldn't agree with that."

"It was awful interesting hearing talk—though it made a kind of sad wedding day."

"Oh, they probably got happy before midnight and forgot all about it."

"Oh, Mr. Howe, how can you!"

After a moment Ben continued airily, "So the deacon is giving them forty acres besides setting them up. It pays to work in town and put up a hard-luck story. Nobody ever gives a poor settler anything!"

Chapter 18

Ann was doing the washing one Saturday in early April as Rollin Forbes came riding madly up the hill on his pony. At the stable he swung down and letting the reins drag hurried toward her. The pony dropped his head and stood panting, his thick winter hair matted with sweat and dust.

"He will take cold in this wind," Ann warned quickly.

"But Miz Howe, I ain't stoppin' only to tell the news—Fort Sumter was all blown to pieces and our flag hauled down—I just come from the telegraph office and that operator fellow just read a telegram from New York!"

Ann rested her dripping hands on the tub. "Oh, Rollin, I'm afraid that means war."

"That's what they did say up town. They think Mr. Lincoln will call for men to put down the rebellion. Me! I'm ready to go tomorrow!"

"But what will your mother say, Rollin? You're so young."

"I'm most eighteen," he exploded, "And I can carry a gun good as any man. But honest, Miz Howe, I got to go. They asked me to ride over past Gid Jardine's and clear to the settlement in Hickory Township. They don't have no telegraph to help keep them posted."

The boy hurried to mount his pony and circling the wind break, galloped along the ridge. As Ann stood at the corner of the house watching the pony and rider recede, she thought of the other young men and what the news might mean to them. There would be John Peck, and Emery, and even Stan. And there would be Lydia's other boy, Francis, and Sarah's Lol. Why, there would be Henry Laurie—and perhaps even Mr. Howe!

At First Church the next day Reverend Heath preached at

length on the crisis in Charleston Harbor—a place that had seemed so far away until now. His plea for tolerance toward "our misguided brothers" and for the turning of the other cheek, fell on deaf ears. People were instead thinking of what might become of the young men and boys among them. Overnight they had become, willingly or not, the pawns of war.

Philo declined her mother's invitation to dinner, saying, "John and I think we had better eat together at our house—while we can."

Outside the meetinghouse folks gathered in small groups. The older men congregated around J. B. Goodell to hear what news he had brought back from Des Moines, where he was in the legislature.

"I know our boys here in Powhatan County will respond to Mr. Lincoln's call when it comes. I heard last night coming home on the stage, he will ask for seventy-five thousand men to put down the rebellion. You men will be needed as soon as Iowa hears what is expected of you—well—er, I mean, expected of us. For now, I would say," he was choosing his words carefully, "you had best keep on here at home. Thank God for the telegraph I worked so hard to get built to our city. Now we can hear as soon as anyone."

Much impressed, a serious-faced beardless youth asked, "What about drilling?"

"Very important—very important. It should begin at once. I shall see what can be done before I return to the capital."

Ben, standing alone at the edge of the crowd, saw Sam Cook elbowing into the crowd dominated by J. B. Goodell. Picking up little Alice and with Ann beside him, they started up the path toward the Barretts.

At supper two weeks later, Ben reported, "They were drilling in Goodell's park when I came past from Blue's store—quite a bunch of them—town men, some farm boys, and I guess most of all the university boys."

"Who was doing it—the commanding, I mean? she asked eagerly.

"You might know it would be Sam Cook! Trying to build himself up to be an officer again. He'd never get elected captain of any company from around here."

"Mrs. Cook is so nice and friendly."

"Men ain't likely to forget Sam defending the horse thief!"

"Mrs. Cook told me last Sabbath that, with his experience, Sam ought to get a major's commission. Poor thing, she says she will have to go home to her folks if Sam goes to war."

"Well, as I started to say—after I'd traded out the butter-and-egg money at Blue's, I drove up the road past the new telegraph office and stopped in front of Lol Phipp's where folks were standing watching the drilling in the park. There was Sam Cook, strutting along ahead of this line of boys, and nary a one of them carrying so much as even a stick for a make-believe gun."

Ann shook her head sadly. "I'm afraid the guns will come later."

"Likely the copperheads got guns already, right down at Blue Knob."

"What is a copperhead, Mr. Howe?"

"It means southern sympathizers—folks that think Lincoln should let the South leave the Union."

"You mean there are folks around Goodell who aren't—loyal?"

"Some look at the thing differently," he said airily.

"Did you see John Peck or Emery and Stan drilling?"

"I saw John. Philo was in the crowd watching. No, your brothers weren't there. Some of us have to stay home to raise crops and beef and pork." Brightening, he added, "Likely pork will be worth better than two-fifty a hundred. I aim to raise more."

Wistfully Ann said, "I feel sorry for John and Philo—being married such a short time and now going to be separated for goodness knows how long."

"It won't be so bad for him with no children and no farm, except that forty your father gave 'em, to worry about. I don't figure the war will last long when Lincoln gets the seventy-five thousand he called for. These Goodell boys are going to form a cavalry troop and ride to war." With a slight sneer he added, "Mr. Goodell saw this coming and bought up enough horses to mount a regiment!"

"But Mr. Howe, he was trying to help."

"Huh, and feathering his own nest, buying them cheap from settlers that don't know they're worth a hundred twenty apiece."

Charley could keep silent no longer, "Will they take our Nellie?"

"Not likely, son."

"Maybe if you have to go," Charley blurted out, "they'd let you bring Nellie to ride."

Ben cast a baleful look at the boy and swallowed hard. He resumed eating in silence. After a few minutes he looked up and said lightly, "You should have seen your friend Gerty Buderfa cutting across the park right while they were drilling—head in the air like she smelled a stink, and never looking to right nor left. Somebody says, 'There goes a copperhead.' I'd just heard at the store about her Jim running off to join the rebels and taking Tom Holt's saddle horse—leastwise they both disappeared about the same time right after Fort Sumter."

"But how could he, Mr. Howe?"

"'Twas easy. Horse was worth a hundred, maybe a hundred twenty."

"I mean, why would he join the rebel army?"

"What else can you expect of a fellow up from Missouri slave country?" Ben said triumphantly.

Poor Gerty, she will have a hard row to hoe with all those children."

After a moment she continued thoughtfully, "I wonder what the Ladies' Benevolent Society will do about Gerty being a copperhead. She was so faithful when I used to sew with them."

"From the way she passed 'em by, I'd say she is content to be left alone."

"Bud is going on sixteen—maybe he can get a job at Clack's mill to help out the family."

"Perhaps, though Clack being an abolitionist he might not want a young copperhead around the mill when the underground hides slaves."

In the midst of those tense spring days of work and worry came a special day when, at breakfast, Ann asked brightly, "Do you know what day this is, Mr. Howe?"

He looked up, startled, wondering.

"It's little Alice's second birthday—and Philo has made her the cutest dress to wear over hoops, and we're going to have her daguerroeotype taken today."

"Well."

"It will make a darling picture," Ann babbled on happily. "They tint the cheeks and even put color in the dress. We are so proud of our little girl, aren't we, Mr. Howe?"

You'd better be thinking about putting in early garden stead of galavantin' off to town having a picture made. You gettin' Charley's taken, too?" he asked, brightening a bit.

"Why no, I hadn't thought of that."

"Well you better remember you've got two children according to what you say. I want the horse today anyway."

Determined not to appear annoyed at his disapproval, she said pleasantly, "Philo is coming for us."

Ben was not the only one around Goodell who felt touchy and upset over war talk. The anxious young men who drilled in the park three afternoons a week were worried day after day lest the war would be over without their ready to help. Enthusiasm ran high. Will Benton who lead the choir of First Church and was quite a musician got together some men who had band instruments tucked away forgotten. A handful of them took to furnishing a little music on drill days.

As spring turned to summer, the band increased in size and their music in quality, after Benton sent clear to Chicago for the latest sheet music, called "We Are Coming, Father Abraham—And Many Thousands More." The words to the piece caught on, and folks humming them gave doubtful young fellows a boost about enlisting. Althought the roster didn't quite fill up, Sam Cook's recruits were anxious to get into service. No one seemed able to get the company accepted. Folks said J.B. Goodell would have known what to do, but he was scarcely ever at home since Fort Sumter. Julia always said he was traveling on business. Rumors were that he was spending a lot of time in Washington City—something about contracts. That was before carpenters began work on the wool warehouse down beyond the new railroad grade.

Discouragement spread among the recruits when word came that the Iowa City Rifles were going into camp. If it hadn't been for Will Benton and the brass band probably a lot more of the boys would have slipped away to enlist. It was hard to see much use in just learning to march in a straight line and form a column of fours when all the time they were sure theirs was going to be a cavalry company.

Word got around meanwhile that Goodell was sending a band whether the cavalry company ever formed or not. Young fellows came to join from prairie towns as much as fifty miles away.

There was talk of uniforms. Goodell would send its band dressed like a band. Lol Phipps was appointed to take the collected money and buy suitable cloth and the braid for the fancy trimming for eighteen men. On his return by stage from Fort Des Moines, even his own wife shook her head in dismay. Her only comment was, "It's good wool cloth." Miss Debbie Hart, self-appointed head of the sewing committee, lighted into the innocent Lol with, "Didn't anybody tell you the rebels are using that color?"

"But I got it worth the money," Lol said defensively, "and he threw in the braid free!"

"Huh, brother Phipps, you got a stinging!"

One evening in early summer, Ann stood in her kitchen door listening intently. From town, borne on a faint breeze, came the shrill notes of a fife and the staccato beat of a snare drum. "I can just barely hear it," she said to Ben coming in with the milk. "Philo said they are having a rally at the meetinghouse to fill out the cavalry company—and Mr. Goodell is making the speech." She listened a moment longer, then turned away, saying, "It is the brass band now—playing the new rally piece, 'Listen to the Mocking Bird.' I kind of wanted to go—to see who volunteers, but I guess you're too tired."

Ben exploded with, "I'd not go across the road to hear old J.B. rant and rave and beg for somebody else to save the Union, not when he's trying to make himself a fortune in wool that the army needs!"

"But Mr. Howe, the town boys—like John—want to fill out—"

"Suppose you let the town tend to itself and you tend to your work here. I'd like a decent supper for a change!"

Ann sighed and turned toward the cookstove.

The week of July Fourth, Ben was breaking prairie for Homer Hanlon. The town celebration, such as it was, would be a picnic in Homer's young grove on the far end of his forty acres. Ann was anxious to go, but Ben, who had no intention of mixing in any patriotic affair, said bitterly, "If you want to go, you'll have to find your own way. I'm not of a mind to eat a cold dinner with that crowd of flag wavers in that pizzling bit of shade. I've been eating my lunch right there every day while my cattle rested—and I'd be there today if it warnt for the crowd."

Ann hitched up Nellie to the buckboard and took Alice and Charley to the celebration—and made excuses for Ben. That was the beginning of another of Ben's gruff, unexplainable spells of silence. It was hard to get used to them. Even the coming of the Sabbath two days later did not change his mood. He refused to go to meeting and curtly declared he needed the horse to go salt the cattle.

As soon as the morning work was done, Ann called in Charley, who was still smarting under an undeserved rebuke from his father, and, taking Alice on her lap, read them Bible stories from the big blue book that had been hers as a child. When Ben returned hours later, she appeared as cheerful and placid as ever.

Ben drew up water from the well and, after washing up, stood motionless looking across the prairie to where his wheat stood tall and straight, motionless in the noonday heat.

Coming to the door, Ann asked anxiously, "Anything wrong?"

"No!"

"You're thinking about the wheat, aren't you? It is so near ripe."

"Yes," he grunted, "today's a weather breeder."

Monday started out much the same. There was a choking breathlessness about the air that even the farm animals noticed. Not long after Ben started to town afoot, banks of angry clouds appeared low in the west. The wind swept them across the leaden sky like a great billowing curtain that brought sudden darkness.

Ann stood outside watching the storm and anxiously scanning the prairie flat for sight of Ben turning back from town. When first the roar of storm could be heard she gathered the children into the house and shut the door.

The fury of the wind increased, and the little house shook and swayed as she stood waiting and praying with Alice in her arms and Charley huddled beside her. Suddenly the boy cried out and pointed to the trap door that led to the cellar. It was raising and flopping as though thrust open by some unseen hand. Putting Alice to the floor screaming, Ann dashed to the bedroom and dragged Ben's leather trunk. Dropping it on the trap door, she sat down with Alice's head buried in her lap and one arm around Charley.

After moments that seemed hours came the rush of colder air, followed by a torrent of rain. Then it was over.

Half an hour later Ben came hurrying across the flat from town. He slowed his pace when he could see that the house still stood and the children were in the yard.

"Did it blow here?" he called as he approached.

Still unnerved, Ann barked at him, "Look at your wheat! Flat like cattle had run through—and part of the stable roof gone! And you ask if it blew here." And she burst into tears.

Charley was trying to get his father's attention, saying excitedly, "And we even had to sit on the trap door to keep out the wind."

"You mean it almost took the house, Charley? Why, you might have been killed!"

Ann had already entered the house thinking, he only worries about the boy—and the wheat.

Chapter 19

"I don't know what we'll do—a man can't cradle wheat when it's flat as a pancake!"

Ben dropped dejectedly on the edge of the well platform and, pulling off his boots, sat scraping off mud with a paddle.

Ann stood in the doorway behind him, waiting.

"Ten acres of it—good wheat it was, too. Likely would of made twenty-five bushels an acre."

"But Mr. Howe, isn't there some way it can be cut?" she asked hesitantly.

"You name it if you know so much," he growled.

"Emery was telling father just the other day—"

"Yes Emery—Emery! You're always quoting Emery!"

"But Mr. Howe," Ann said patiently, "It was about saving the wheat."

"Let's hear it, then."

"He said Abner Smith is bringing one of those new-fangled harvesters to town. He says it can cut right down to the ground and that a man rakes the wheat off the platform to the ground into piles for men to bind, just like behind the cradlers."

She sounded enthusiastic.

After a minute Ben said skeptically, "I don't think much of these new-fangled machines." After a pause he continued stoically, "It's just another scheme to get rich off us poor settlers. Likely Abner would want all the grain was worth just to cut it.

"Lydia Forbes told me even before the cyclone that Will was going to hire Abner and his machine to cut his."

"Huh, I can't figure Will being so free-handed with money— him with two boys to cradle for him for nothing."

"She said Abner charged only fifty cents an acre."

"I won't pay it!"

"But Mr. Howe, Lydia says wheat is worth sixty cents a bushel at the railroad—and it's only thirty miles now to the end of steel."

Three days later, Abner Smith drove into the farm yard with the bright red machine. As he applied tallow to the working parts he paused to ask, "How many acres in the piece you want harvested?" holding the last word as though with pride.

"Looks like hardly ten acres," Ben offered cannily, "The way the slough cuts off the lower corner. I figured four dollars'd be about right."

Abner straightened up and noticed the tangled swath the storm had cut across the field. "My God, Ben, you didn't tell me it was in that shape. I ought to get seventy-five cents an acre!"

"You never asked me if it stood straight," Ben declared craftily. Then he added his final argument: "Five dollars is a lot of money."

Abner stopped the greasing and leaned languidly against the harvester. His easy indifference worried Ben, who swallowed hard and said in an almost apologetic tone, "I guess I should have told you how it lay, Abner, but I never did see one of these things and how was I to know it made a difference."

"I've got to pay a hundred fifty dollars for this here harvester before snow flies—and this young fellow gits fifty cents a day just to rake the grain off'n the platform while I drive the team. But if you say the word, I'll cut it," Abner conceded.

"Sure. Go ahead." And Ben heaved an inward sigh of relief.

As soon as the little red machine started circling the wheat, Ben dragged Charley from play and made it plain to him that he was to be water boy and no foolishness. "I don't want them men having to come to the well for a drink—it takes time. And when you aren't doing the water you drag them bundles into piles for shocking."

"But Mr. Howe, aren't there apt to be rattlesnakes under the bundles?" Ann remonstrated.

"Could be," Ben replied indifferently, "but he can learn to watch."

From the doorway she watched the boy cautiously approach each bundle and peer fearfully beneath before dragging it to a pile. If I could only understand Mr. Howe—he dotes so on the child at times and then cares nothing about him—like he does toward me.

Two weeks later, with the precious wheat safe in four big stacks to wait for the threshing machine, a peaceful quiet settled over the farm. Even the war seemed remote there. But to John Peck and the other young men still drilling regularly, tension mounted. They resented the delay in filling up the company and being mustered into service.

Since Fort Sumter, Ben had secretly worried over the war, perhaps foreseeing better than many that it would drag on for years to some bitter truce. Early he had realized he might be called to serve. He tried to believe he was too old.

Ann had tried for a long time to understand Ben's indifference toward slavery. Now she was further baffled by his aversion toward anything pertaining to the war. She had been quick to notice he evaded being in town on drill days, after that first time in April when he had reported Sam Cook was commanding. She wondered now what he would think if he knew Henry Laurie, now a clerk in Mike Sydon's private bank, had taken charge of the drilling.

Neither had Ann ever mentioned she had been in town the day the brass band left for the army. The whole town had turned out to see them, resplendent in their gray uniforms, fill two stages drawn up at Chapin's tavern. The bandman had taken a lot of chaffing about their uniforms—and given a lot right back at the cavalry boys who were still waiting to be called.

When at last the stages were loaded and started west out of town, there was plenty calling after them, "Hey, the war is down this other way," though everyone knew they were going to join the Fourth Iowa Volunteer Regiment forming at Council Bluffs.

Chapter 20

Ann was sitting by the fire, as she had been most of the day since Ben went early to the timber. engrossed in putting a patch on the knee of Charley's wool pants, she looked up in surprise as the clock struck. Doing the mending was a strange way to spend Thanksgiving, she was thinking.

It was quiet in the house save for the slow ticking of the clock and the wood crackling in the round heating stove. Alice was asleep in her trundle bed and Charley was with his father.

All of her troubles bore down upon her at once—Charley so impudent, so independent and hard to manage—Ben so moodily silent, so bitterly critical of whatever she said or did. She had long since resigned herself to a spiritless marriage in which she gave all of herself and received nothing in return. For her there was no real joy in marriage, save that it had brought her little Alice. The child was the one bright spot in her life.

She tried to shake off her mounting despair by planning for the child. Her years of growing up—her clothing—her schooling. Why, perhaps she could go to Goodell University! Then a strange premonition came over her. What if something awful happened to Alice? She put down her mending and hurried to where the child slept. Satisfied, she turned away thinking perhaps it was mother sick—or father. She went to the window to peer out for sight of some messenger hurrying across the flat. It was all so plain—some danger, some threat to someone of those she loved. Maybe it was Mr. Howe hurt in some accident in the timber—or Charley. She shouldn't have let him go.

She continued to feel restless and uneasy until Ben returned from the timber at dusk with Charley running gaily beside the oxen.

So perhaps it was John Peck, sick at camp in eastern Iowa. In vain she tried to reason that what was to be would be, yet the uncanny dread continued.

During the days Ann's dream seemed most real, Ben was moody and silent. She wondered if he, too, had had some premonition. He never spoke except to answer some pleading of Alice's, or one of Charley's interminable questions. At the table Ann often eyed him critically as he sat stirring endlessly at his coffee. His face did look drawn and bitter above the ragged line of bushy whiskers. Perhaps he, too, had some nameless fears of danger or tragedy.

To break the silence she asked cheerily, "Can you guess what Alice weighs on Harve Blue's scales, Mr. Howe?"

"No."

"She weighs thirty-one pounds—isn't that grand?"

"Was it on the scales Harve buys over?" he asked cannily.

"And what do you think I weighed?" she asked eagerly.

"I can't guess," he said listlessly.

"A hundred and nineteen! Now you know what a big eater I am," she said gaily. "You weigh as much as both of us, don't you?"

"Perhaps."

He finished his coffee, rose hurriedly, and, without a word, slipped on his boots and work frock. From the window she watched him going to the stable. His shoulders drooped dejectedly. Poor man, she thought, perhaps he is coming down with consumption like Laura.

Beside the strange dread that still haunted her, Ben's mounting discouragement made matters worse. His eyes were haggard at times, and his unexplained silences, his always bitter discouragement, and his talk, what little he made, betrayed his worries. He made bitter references to the thieving railroads driving still lower the price of wheat—and the weather always appeared threatening, or there was sure to come a big snow and make wood cutting impossible—then they's all freeze.

Once when his discouragement seemed greatest, she tried to make his troubles lighter by recounting her own. "Imagine Harve Blue allowing me six cents a pound in trade for butter. Think of the time I spent churning." She laughed gaily. "And there I was, planning to buy some new ribbons for my old brown bonnet with what was left!"

He looked up in surprise as she babbled on: "and the eggs brought five whole cents a dozen!"

Ben's stern dark look returned. "This is no time for gewgaws. Anyway, you'd better let me do the tradin' with Blue."

"I even thought I wanted some ruching to fix up my second-best dress—but then, we have so much to be thankful for, don't we?"

Her voice had such a happy lilt that for a moment he was almost ashamed of his own dark moods. After all, she does make a home for me—and Charley—though she would never be the hand that Laura was.

Clad in her warmest clothing plus a work frock of Ben's for good measure, Ann stood in the lee of the house and woodshed peering hopefully into the swirling snow toward the stable. She was drumming endlessly on a big syrup cooking pan. The snow, hard frozen in the subzero cold, driven by a galelike wind, swept down over the roofs, stinging her face and nearly smothering her. Through that gray curtain of snow Ben had disappeared almost an hour ago to do a few stable chores.

For once he had stayed indoors after dinner, sitting silently, restlessly watching the storm worsen. As the clock struck four he had risen and gone out, barking a refusal to Charley's plea to go along.

Ann had watched him wade through the drift at the corner of the woodshed and then drop out of sight as the storm closed its curtains behind him. As she watched the old recurring dread of disaster gripped her.

She had gone back to knitting but made no progress. Little Alice had awakened from her nap and later joined Charley at the kitchen window where they shared the narrowing clear spot in the frost watching for their father.

The clock struck the three-quarter hour as Charley called, "I can't see the stable or even the chicken house, and it's getting worse."

"Well, you keep watching and pretty soon you'll see your father coming, and then I'll get supper and we will be all safe and warm even if it is storming outside."

Her words were intended to reassure herself as well as the children. For a few minutes she sat with her knitting forgotten in her lap. Stories of settlers lost and frozen to death on the prairie came to haunt her. She remembered the storm that first winter with Emery and Stan going out hand over hand along a rope to guide them back. But Mr. Howe had nothing to guide him—no one but her.

With swift determination she had dressed warmly and hurried to the door. Alice began to cry and Charley, turning from the window, shrilled, "I want to go."

Catching him by the shoulder, she whirled him around, screaming at him, in a tone he had not heard before, with every word bitten short through tight-set lips: "Young man, you stay here and don't you dare to leave this house—and keep the fire going and get you two something to eat—if I don't come back!"

"Aren't you coming back?" the child whimpered.

She slammed the door without answering, thinking, I wish I knew!

Now, fifteen minutes later, stamping her feet against the creeping chill, she kept drumming on the big pan and alternately clattering the old hand bell. The hollow moan and roar of the storm deadened the sounds just as it muffled her voice when she tried shouting for Ben.

In desperation, she pushed her way beyond the woodshed, determined to reach the stable and search for him. After a dozen plodding steps she glanced back. In the gathering gloom the dim outline of the shed had almost faded away. Frightened, she staggered back into the lee of the building, dazed and battered by the exposure.

She tried to think if she dared to leave the children, but the answer was always the same—I've got to find Mr. Howe—help him to find the house—he's all I've got. Fiercely she resumed drumming.

She imagined he was calling her, first from one direction then from another as the storm eddied around the buildings. He is trying to find me—maybe crawling—drowsy—exhausted and freezing.

She took up the bell again.

Meanwhile, Ben had hurried through his chores, milked and fed the small calves, and filled mangers. Then with head bent low, he opened the stable door and began struggling waist-deep in snow. Smothering and breathless from exertion, he stopped to rest his back to the wind. In that brief moment all sense of direction vanished. He felt as though he was adrift in the center of a whirlpool of snow.

Cautiously he tried to retrace the dozen or more steps he had taken, but the wind had filled full the tracks he had made. Numbed and dizzy from the swirling snow, he realized his own danger, for the shadow of the stable had disappeared.

Confused and defeated, he stood listening, listening for some sound, something to guide him to the house. With a mittened hand he raised his heavy cap from one ear. It's likely only the wind, he thought, there'd be no sound from the house. Or was that real—that rhythmic beating always the same, faint above the roar and whine of the wind?

He staggered a few steps toward it. The wind played tricks with the drumming sound echoing it back and forth. Then he heard it clearer, followed by a tinkling sound. Desperately holding to his position, he tried to brush the snow from his eyes and as he did, saw a faint flicker of light.

Dazed and unbelieving, he staggered ahead and struck against a building. It was clapboarded. Slowly he inched his way along. The wall ended, and he groped his way back to the corner. Hand over hand he continued to a window at which a candle flickered feebly. A few feet farther and there stood Ann, white with snow still drumming and ringing. He staggered toward her, and she grabbed him, pulling him into the kitchen.

Sitting before the cookstove with his feet propped on the oven door, Ben looked slowly around the room as though unbelievng. His eyes followed Ann as she hovered about him. His hand shook as he held the heavy cup of tea to his lips.

It was some time before he spoke haltingly between gulps, "I must have got clear away—out in the open—beyond the buildings. I was done for—ready to give up—then I heard the noise you made. You saved me."

"It was little enough I did," Ann said in a low tone. "You are all I've got—you and the children.

He put up an arm and drew her to him. Charley and little Alice had stood back watching wide-eyed. Charley sensing the seriousness of it all said manfully, "I was keeping the fire going while Aunt Ann was outside. I was scared, but I didn't let sister know—and I lighted the candle in the other window for you, Father."

For two nights and a day while the storm raged over them, the four seemed drawn as close as though marooned on some lonely isle. Ben was more amiable than for many months. He seemed to unlimber for once and in the evening sat contentedly beside the stove in the sitting room, cracking hickory and hazel nuts for them all. Even Alice shared in his attention, sitting on his lap and talking away by the hour. Charley watched his father closely in this new role of a pleasant and entertaining parent. The second evening they gathered around the cookstove watching Anne cooking the batch of molasses.

"I declare, Mr. Howe," she said and laughed gaily, "you are in as much of a hurry for the candy as the children are. Remember, it has to cool first.

When she handed him a wad of the stuff to pull, he took it willingly enough and smiled as he said, "I've not pulled any molasses candy since I was young—at Laura's house, back east."

For a moment his eyes had a far-away look. Then he roused himself and called to Ann to rescue him when he got tangled up with the rope of yellowish sticky stuff that was a bit too soft. The children watching intently as the two set about pulling the batch, hand to hand, back and forth, doubling and pulling till it was lighter in color and hardening fast. Alice giggled when her father licked his fingers for what molasses stuck to them.

Oh, if we could only stay like this, Ann thought, the four of us so happy together. Perhaps this storm was the something I dreaded. Soon it will be over, and we are going to be all right.

Chapter 21

John Peck sat in the Howe's sitting room dangling little Alice on his knee. His attention was centered on the child, though he was trying to answer some of Ann's questions. No, the storm had not been so bad at Camp Harlan in east Iowa. Yes, the snow blew clear through the wooden barracks, but they just shoveled it out. No, they'd not get cavalry horses till they went south in the spring.

When Philo claimed little Alice, John continued, with a sly smile: "Philo thinks I'm next thing to being an officer like Sam Cook. Well, I haven't slipped any—I'm still sixth corporal!"

"I think he must have been in some mischief, the way he acts," Philo said gaily.

"At least I've never sneaked past the guards to get into Mount Pleasant. Most of the young fellows make it regular."

He glanced proudly toward Philo. "Being a married man, I'm not interested in what the boys find in those shanties off limits."

The two women at once became intent on something Alice was doing, and did not look up. His frankness amazed them.

At four, Philo insisted on starting home. "I've got boarders to get supper for, you know."

"Yes," John said jovially, "as soon as I went to camp she took in half a dozen to feed, and she claims she feeds them for the same money she spent for the two of us."

"Well, I had to help out by doing something. Besides, waiting doesn't seem so bad if I'm busy." She laughed. "John's thirteen dollars a month didn't go far."

"Who are you boarding now?" Ann asked.

"The same ones I had—the two teachers, Ray Clack the daguerreotypist and the new dentist, Dr. Pulitzer—and you never could guess my latest addition—it's Henry Laurie!"

"He's courting Postmaster Spensley's daughter three nights a week. I don't think he is going to volunteer," Philo added lamely.

"It's just like Mr. Howe says so often—that it takes men to stay at home to keep things running. I expect Mike Sydon needs Henry in the bank," Ann apologized.

Their sleigh had passed from sight when Ben entered the house and asked quite innocently, "Did you have company for tea?"

"I was so in hopes you'd come in while they were here. It was John and Philo. I was almost sure you must have seen them when they drove up."

"No, I guess I didn't."

"John asked about you several times. He always did like you."

"He can see me some other time."

"Maybe not, because he just has a veteran's furlough—ten days. He thinks he is going to like the cavalry."

"Cavalry, huh! I hear they haven't got horses yet. I wonder what became of all the cavalry horses old J. B. Goodell had bought up. He had enough for a regiment. I tell you, I don't figure this war will last long after John and the Fourth Cavalry get down there to help Sam Cook clean out the secess mob."

He picked up the milk bucket and started out, then turned to say glumly, "A. P. Coker was past here—yesterday it was—and he wanted me to take Gilbert to chore and help out till spring, for his board."

"But Mr. Howe, Gilbert isn't even very bright!"

"Well, I figure he can do chores. I want to haul some sixty-cent wheat to the railroad," he added cynically, "and it will take me three days with oxen."

Gilbert Coker proved to be much as Ann had anticipated. An overgrown simple-minded youth, near man-grown in size, he was awkward and irresponsible as a child. His stolid resignation to the dull monotony of heavy work won him Ann's sympathy at first.

As a chore boy, Gilbert's industriousness was short-lived. Without Ben to remind him of what to do, he left the chores to follow Charley in his play after returning from school. Then Ann would bundle herself up and, leaving Alice alone in the house, would go out to keep the youth at his work. Exasperated, she even climbed the stack and began throwing down hay to the cattle. Gilbert, finally noticing, reluctantly tore himself away from helping Charley make a sled.

"I plum forgot about the hay, Miz Howe," he drawled.

Ann handed him the fork, thinking—it's bad enough having a husband gone so much—and then to have a trifling boy to watch every minute.

Near bedtime the third day, Ben's heavy sled came creaking across the snow and pulled up at the stable. Ann hurried to poke up the fire in the cookstove. When he entered he appeared surprised to find her waiting, with the coffee pot simmering and his place at the table set. She edged the bootjack along the floor toward him, then pulled a chair to the stove and opened the oven door.

"Sit here and warm you feet," she commanded, "while I get you a hot drink."

Ben did not speak. He seemed too numb and dazed with weariness.

Watching him while busy at the stove heating food for his late supper, a new feeling of tenderness and sympathy came over her. He looks so tired and discouraged, so cold and fagged out—going farther with the wheat to get such a little more. I shouldn't complain at doing a few chores, she thought.

She handed him the heavy cup and stood for a moment with an arm about his shoulder while he began sipping noisily. After a little while he asked in a thin voice, "Did you get along all right—with Gilbert to chore?"

"Don't worry about us here at home," she said lightly. "What kind of a trip did you have—and where did you stay last night?"

"In a cabin this side of Marengo—wido woman runs the place," he said, then added, "Packed in like sardines in a keg."

She looked at him sharply, but said only, "You had to walk beside the cattle to keep warm, didn't you?"

"Every step of the way—forty miles and facing the wind," he replied weakly.

"My sakes, I hope you're not going to haul any more wheat now. Alice spent hours at the window watching for you."

At breakfast next morning Ben announced he was going to town to build a light sled at Koepke's wagon shop, adding, "So we can get some good out of our one horse."

"Oh, that will be nice. I've been wishing for one. Will you get it done today, before chore time?" she asked, thinking he would have a chance to observe Gilbert's choring.

"Huh, you don't have much of an idea what a job it is to make a sled—blacksmithing and all," he said scornfully. "Yes, I think I'll be home."

Two days passed, and there was no word from Ben. Ann was fast losing interest in any sled that took so long to build. She suspected he was loafing and not working. She was quite sure he would not go to Barretts for lodging. Where was he staying?

By midafternoon of the third day of Ben's venture, her doubts and fears compelled action. She called Charley from play and sent him afoot to look for his father. Then she started the slow-moving Gilbert to choring. At early dusk when neither Ben nor Charley had returned, she sent Gilbert after the both of them astride the horse, slyly sending along the light harness—"For Mr. Howe to bring home the sleigh."

An hour later she heard Ben and the two boys at the stable. From the window she could see they had brought home the sled. Later, when they came hurrying in to supper, she gave no sign of elation at Ben's return and was matter-of-fact about it.

Ben was more talkative than usual, bringing the latest news of the town and firsthand reports of camp life as retold, no doubt around the stove at the wagon shop. As fast as one subject was exhausted he launched into another.

Ann listened with mild interest. She was making a certain strong resolve of her own.

Ten days later, when Ben announced he was taking another load of wheat to the railroad, Ann had something of her own to say.

"I feel like I was coming down with a very bad cold," she said with a new firmness in her voice. "Alice and I are going to ride to town with you and stay at Father's. Charley can stay there, too."

Ben looked surprised.

"I thought you'd be here to look after things," he said petulantly.

"Gilbert can do the chores," she said lightly, wondering if he would.

So for three days Ann rested and relaxed at Stephen's while Philo made her two dresses from cloth Doshia "just happened to have in the house."

When Ben returned he stood at the door, restless, as Ann picked up her sewing. Watching him, she wondered why he should be so anxious to get home when he was so willing to stay away.

Homeward bound as they approached Sam Woodburn's at the edge of the townsite, Ann clutched Ben's sleeve saying, "Oh, please do wait while I go in to see how Mary is."

"Well," grudgingly, "what ails her?"

"The doctors don't know. Philo heard at the post office this very afternoon it's some kind of fever—maybe from the camps. Mary is burning with fever and wrenching terrible with vomiting."

"Sounds like poison," Ben observed casually. "I heard long ago Sam was wanting to move her out west, but she wouldn't go. I never thought Sam would want to go that bad, though!"

As Ann climbed back into the sled, Ben turned to her and said sternly, "You shouldn't have gone in there! If it ain't poisoning it might be catchin' and you'd give it to Charley—or even Alice."

"But Mr. Howe, Sarah Phipps is in there helping."

"Yes, but she's no weakling catchin' everything that comes."

The next morning Asa Burrell's oldest boy brought word that Mary Woodburn died before midnight. He added, with awe in his voice, "And they say she was covered with bloody spots under her skin."

Spotted fever!

Chapter 22

Two weeks later, Ben left the oxen and sled standing by the Barrett stable and hastened toward the house. Stephen met him at the kitchen door and said in hushed tones. "She has been awful sick. Ben — we've been expecting you back from Marengo since yesterday. Her bad cold turned into a high fever the same day you left, and even Dr. Harbaugh thought it was spotted fever!"

"So she had fever again, did she? Ben asked, quite undisturbed. "She did seem a little under the weather. Are you sure it wasn't the ague?"

"Mother and Philo stayed with her day and night to keep her quiet till the fever burned out. She was clear out of her head for quite a while, Ben."

"I told her not to go to Mary Woodburn's funeral — told her it might be catching. Are you sure it wasn't just the ague, sir?"

"Doc Harbaugh called in Tom Holt, and they both thought sure it was this new plague," Stephen argued.

"You mean she had to have two doctors?" Ben asked incredulously.

"You have no idea how bad this epidemic is, Ben They buried two more today. That makes eight since Mary Woodburn."

"Then Ann would be better off at the farm away from all these sick people," Ben said triumphantly.

"We will have to see what her mother says about that," Stephen said firmly.

As Ben entered the sickroom Ann tried to sit up and speak, but slumped back again.

"So you are still a little sick, are you?" he demanded. "I was just saying you'd be better off at home. Get dressed, and as soon as Charley comes from school, we'll go."

No one moved.

He continued, "It took me longer because I had to wait in line to shovel my load into a freight car—and then I waited for hours for the dealer to get money to pay. I was in a hurry, too, account of spring coming and I've got so much to do—more wood to cut and butchering for summer meat."

Apparently he was keeping up this rapid-fire talk to cover up Ann's delay in obeying his order to dress. As he paused, Doshia straightened up from her patient and, putting her hands on her hips, said with grim determination, "Mr. Howe, Ann is not going home to a cold house to take care of herself or help with the butchering—and her not able to hold her head up!"

"It's likely nothing but a touch of the ague." His tone had changed, for he said quite calmly, "I just as well be going. I'll have to put off the butchering."

As he turned to go downstairs, Doshia forced herself to call after him pleasantly, "Stop in for a meal anytime you're in town."

A week later, at her own insistence, Ann went home. As Philo drove her across the slough and started up the hill toward the house, Ann exclaimed, "See there, my work is waiting for me!" Three hog carcasses dangled from the end of the stable roof.

He couldn't wait till you got some strength, could he?" Philo sputtered.

Ann shook her head sadly. "Poor man, he frets so about getting things done when spring comes. I'll manage some way, only this time it's going to be harder."

Ann stooped to push fresh wood under the big iron kettle, and the fire brightened, sending the smoke curling across the sundappled door yard, dimming for a moment the bright April sun. Cautiously she touched the steaming water and, finding it right for the washing, called cheerily, "Charley, come help mother just a little, please."

The boy stood at the stable door looking up at the pigeons in the loft, a slingshot in his hand. She called again, and in a flash he darted around the corner.

She stood for a moment, bucket in hand, glancing toward the wooden tubs set against the woodshed, and wished the water was in them and the kettle refilled for the rinsing.

Once more she called pleadingly, "Please, Charley, you help Mother just a little and I'll bake something you like, soon as I get done here."

She saw the boy peering impishly around the corner of the

stable, then disappear. Wearily she dipped a bucketful and carried it fifty feet to the tubs.

At midmorning Ben came hurryingly along the ridge from the back forty, where he had been sowing by hand. Ann was sitting dejectedly on the well platform as he approached.

"You ain't done washing yet?" he scolded. "And it's almost time to start dinner."

"I know I'm slow," she said in patient tones. "I get so tired carrying so much water I can scarce stand to work."

"Why don't you get Charley to tote the water? All you have to do is ask him."

She got up and leaned heavily against the tub, her voice rising. "That is the same way you do. You never help me. You wouldn't care if I'd died from the fever like they thought I was going to. I tell you, I'm sick — sick — "

"Well, you don't need to scream about it. Other women work. Land sakes, what can I do with the boy? He behaves when I'm here. You just ain't the hand with him that—"

Ann rushed across the piazza and disappeared into the house. Ben stood looking down at his own soapy, bedraggled work clothes slumped across the washboard. He leaned over and gave them a trial rub on the board, then thought better of it and poked the slimy mess under the water. As he stood wiping his hands on his breeches, he glanced around cautiously. Alice stood in the door holding her rag doll.

"You going to do Mama's washing, father?"

"No, of course not!"

"What you going to do, then?"

"I'm going to take Nellie and harrow in the wheat!"

Two hours later when he came to dinner, Ann had somehow finished the washing, and the meal was ready. He looked critically at the table. "Huh! Beans and pork again. You know I like a change. A man followin' a harrow all day needs something fit to eat."

"Then you are done seeding," she said, cutting off the threatened tirade.

"It's about time. This is the twenty-fifth of April. We'll never make a crop seeded this late," he declared dismally.

"Then you are using Nellie to harrow — I was going to take the eggs and butter to town to trade out."

He made no reply but began eating rapidly.

In the silence that followed came the sound of rapid hoof beats. Ann rose and went to look.

"Why, it's Asa Burrell's oldest boy—and in a hurry, looks like."

"Wish I wasn't to home," Ben grumbled nervously. "Likely old Asa either wants help to get his crop in—or there's something the matter."

The boy swung off and hastened toward the house. His face was, for once, not wreathed in smiles.

"I just come from town," he blurted, "and Rollin Forbes died in camp way down south somewheres. I figured you'd want to know."

"Poor Lydia—poor Lydia," was all Ann could say. She stood leaning against the open door watching the boy ride out across the ridge toward home.

She turned to look across the prairie to Forbes's tiny unpainted house on the other road. As she took her place at the table again she said, "I'd go over there to be with her, if I wasn't so tired. Poor Lydia—"

"You'd do better to get your own work done than goin' sympathizin' with the neighbors," Ben said tartly.

"We never know where death or trouble will hit, do we, Mr. Howe?"

The next day Ann stopped at Stephen's for a short visit after doing her trading at Shute's. While there she became feverish. When put to bed the fever rose even higher. As Dr. Harbaugh examined her, Stephen and Doshia stood silently watching, fearful he would find the bloody splotches that had marked the other victims. Instead the young doctor brusquely ordered heated bricks and warm blankets. "We've got to break this fever. Don't give her any water if you can resist her begging for it."

At the door he turned to say, "I think you should send for her husband. This is no light attack like she had before."

Ann's delerium was at its height when Ben finally arrived. She lay moaning and tossing, begging for water and crying pitifully, "Alice, please Alice, help Mother find Charley—I've got to do the chores!" As Ben approached the bed she looked at him blankly, moaning, "Help me find Charley—he's run away again."

Ben stood silently a moment, ignoring her groping hand.

"Ann—Ann, you've got to get hold of yourself," he said sharply, as though gruffness would bring her back to reality.

Doshia turned away and stood at the window unseeing, her

hands clenched beneath her apron.

As Ben clumped noisily down the steps and across the sitting room, Stephen, sitting dejectedly by the kitchen table, rose to say, "We will do all we can, Ben." The old man's voice broke.

Ben paused only long enough to say quite calmly, "I'm sure of that, so I guess I'll be going—it's a pretty busy time for me."

The fever left its mark on Ann. Ten days later, when first she was dressed, her speech was thick and her vision impaired. "Partial paralysis," Dr. Harbaugh pronounced it. "If she can rest and build up her strength she may regain her sight and the use of her right hand and leg."

During the later days of her sickness, Stephen found and hired Christine, a buxom German immigrant girl, to help Doshia. She would go with Ann to the farm when she recovered. But the recovery would be dreadfully slow.

Two days later after Ann left her sickbed, Ben demanded bitterly that she return home, ending with, "You've been away too long now, and with Christine to—"

"But Mr. Howe," Ann mumbled feebly, attempting to rise.

"I said it's time you came with me. Here I am, slaving away trying to get the corn planted alone and cooking my own meals. Tain't fair—I have my rights." He was looking at the buxom Crhistine, thinking—if the deacon will keep paying her, it looks like a good deal for me.

At the farm the young and tireless girl won Ben's outspoken praise by thriftily planting the garden and, when that was done, turned to cleaning the house. Through it all Ann could only watch from her bed.

But the girl's cooking was a disappointment to Ben, for she served him strange German dishes and when he ate sparingly, she served it as leftovers. She added to his growing indignation by regarding him coldly when they were alone.

A week after Ann's return home, Ben rose disgustedly from the breakfast table and entered the bedroom.

"I tell you I've got to have something fit to eat," he roared. "I can't stand it another day. Other women don't lay in bed and let a blathering foreigner feed their man trash!"

"But Mr. Howe, she will hear you," Ann murmured feebly.

"She couldn't understand anyway because when I tell her what I want she looks at me dumblike. I want pie once in a while. And maybe doughnuts. Something fit to eat. But I suppose you're too sick to do anything about it."

Once unleashed, Ben's tirade covered all Ann's mistakes and failures. She was lazy, extravagant, and not a fit wife for a poor settler struggling to get a start. And besides, she was a plain fool to get exposed to the dratted fever anyway.

Ann lay with eyes closed to shut out the sight of him towering over her as his abuse mounted. She knew Charley would be hearing it all and gloating over every bitter word hurled at her.

Then came his final words, sarcastic and biting: "And no wonder he still calls you Aunt Ann. You're not a fit mother to him. You're not the hand with him that Laura was!"

The kitchen door slammed.

Ann lay as though stunned, with eyes closed to shut out the world that seemed to be crashing down about her. She was trying to clear her mind and plan her course. He only wanted a woman to bring up Charley—and keep house. I've failed, she thought. But I won't go home to father's. If it kills me I'll do my part.

Resolutely she struggled up from her bed, dressed, and, with Christina holding her up, she hobbled to the kitchen. Propped in a chair she rolled out pie crusts, mixed a gingerbread, and made doughnuts, with the girl tending to the baking and frying.

Later, as Ann dropped wearily into bed, she murmured bitterly, "Now I hope Mr. Howe is satisfied!"

Chapter 23

The trace chains jingled rhythmically with each step Nellie took as Ben led her up the hill from the spring. Little Alice, darting across the piazza and down the path toward the stable, flinched as the heat of the midday July sun on the hard-packed earth stung her bare feet. Disconsolately, she dangled a dilapidated corn-husk doll.

"Mr. Booker," she drawled in childish wistfulness, "I want another dolly—this one is all broke."

The old man straightened up and started toward the stable with his armful of ear corn. "I can't make you another till your paw and me get the corn plowed again. Or maybe after supper."

"Please, Mr. Booker," she lisped. But the rest of her plea was lost in her father's lusty shouts for Charley to come help stable the horse. It irked him that Alice had not even noticed him, but had run straight to the hired man—and besides, the boy wasn't there to help!

He called again. No answer.

"Never mind, Ben, boys will be boys. I'll halter your horse and feed 'em both. It's no chore."

Ben started to the house rolling up his sleeves as he went. Tossing his hat on the piazza, he sat down to pull off his boots.

"Ann—Ann," he demanded loudly, "where's Charley?"

She came to the door and peered out calmly, saying sweetly, "Why, Mr. Howe, I guess he has run away again. Seems like I haven't seen him since early this forenoon when I was starting to carry my wash water."

Ben looked up over his shoulder and scowled as he said with increasing irritation. "Did you call him or ring the bell?"

"Oh no, I was so sure he was hoeing corn for you. He does love to help you so," she said in honeyed tones of deliberate sarcasm.

Ben stood up, shading his eyes, sweeping the prairie for sight of

Charley's bobbing figure. Then he turned and, dipping water from the rain barrel, began washing, blowing his nose vigorously.

At dinner Ben was silent and dejected, while old Henry was talkative. That saved Ben from saying anything to Ann about the boy, or anything else, for that matter. The old man's voice trailed on monotonously, with Ann saying only "Yes" and "No," and "Well I declare." Evidently, the old man drifted around the country considerable and heard lots of news and rumors. Ben paid no attention until he heard the words "Blue Knob" and "Copperhead."

"There's a nest of copperheads down in that neck of the woods," Henry was saying. "I come through there last week—stopped at a house—shanty was all it was—young feller name of Gleasner lived there."

Ben brightened at the name.

"Well, I passed the time of day with him—talked about gettin' out saw logs for a horse power mill—kept thinking he'd ask me in to eat. Finally I said something about the war goin' pretty good for the Union boys. That set him off. The feller just blazed. He swore—no, ma'am, I'l not repeat what he said. You can always tell a copperhead. Just mention a Union victory—or talk about the draft."

"The draft!" Ben echoed in utter amazement, fork in midair.

"Yep," old Henry continued complacently, "the Iowa City paper says there's going to be a draft, maybe this fall yet."

"Well I hadn't heard that," Ben said dumbfounded.

Ann, sitting across the table, watched him shift uncomfortably in his chair and even cease his hurried eating as Henry explained, "They're going to sign up all men from twenty to forty-five. Let's see, that'd ketch you, wouldn't it, Ben?"

"I'm most forty-two," he replied in level tones, not knowing whether to rejoice at the fact or regret it.

"That lets me out—I'm fifty-one! But take a young feller like you, Ben, you got good feet and good teeth to bite off them paper cartridges they use."

Ann interrupted, seeking to change the subject that embarrassed Ben. "But what will happen if the men who are drafted don't come?"

"Gov'ment will go get 'em."

After that conversation lagged. When dinner was over, Ben hastened to intercept some settler coming up the hill from the creek crossing. Ann watched him standing beside the wagon, one foot on the wheel, as he talked earnestly with the man on the seat. She waited and saw Ben shake his head, sadly it seemed, and taking a last look down the trail, turn and hurry toward the stable.

His sudden concern for the boy raised no sympathy in her. It was Ben's turn to worry. He sensed her determination to ignore the little runaway, and he kept silent, blaming her indifference to "that little spell of fever she had."

It was three weeks later, while Ann was pottering around in the garden that she saw the wanderer, silhouetted against the sky, trudging along the ridge from the west. She decided it would be better to show no delight or even surprise at his return, though the decision was a hard one to make.

Her greeting was as casual as though he was returning from an hour of play. She stood blocking the kitchen door, noticing most his tattered clothes and his grimy feet. She asked no questions. He was anxious to volunteer information.

"I guess they told you I been at Branson's over in the Hickory Grove settlement," he began.

"Why no, I hadn't heard," she said quite indifferently.

After a moment he said wearily, "I sure hoed a lot of potatoes, and weeded corn for him—just days and days."

She didn't appear to be listening even then. He continued, hopeful of a little sympathy. "I slept in the corn crib—their house was full. Mrs. Branson ain't the cook you are, Aunt Ann."

To all of this her only comment was, "Well, I declare."

Then as if to justify his adventure, he proudly produced a paper dollar Mr. Branson had given him.

"That was nice of him, but of course, you know a paper dollar is only worth about sixty or seventy cents now."

Turning to Alice, who stood cluthcing her mother's skirts, peering around at the wanderer, she said, "Go get the real dollar you earned and show that to Charley."

The boy's eyes widened at the tiny gold piece clutched in the hand of the three-year-old.

"How did you earn that?" he demanded.

"I kissed a man," she lisped bashfully.

"That is right. We were sitting here on the edge of the piazza one evening, watching the fireflies in the slough, and old Mr. Booker, who works here now, offered her the piece for a kiss. So she got up her courage. It was a quick one, but he paid."

"Huh," Charley grunted disgustedly, wadding his dollar back into his pocket without another look.

The boy seemed restless as conversation dragged. This was not the reception he had expected.

"You'd better see your father," Ann suggested firmly. "He is over beyond town breaking sod for Gideon Merritt. It's only two or three miles."

Charley looked disappointed. He thought of the five long dusty miles he had walked since Mrs. Branson's none-to-savory breakfast. Now he was expected to walk three more miles. He began to wonder what "The old man," as he was secretly calling him, would say.

Ann stood at the door and watched him start reluctantly down past the stable, jump the run below the spring and start across the flat to find his father. For days she had steeled herself against the time he would come crawling back to his home to worm his way into her good graces. She felt she had resisted well. His return served only to remind her that she had already paid dearly for believing that he needed her. She had lost both the boy and his father.

Resolutely she turned away and limped slowly to the garden and took up her hoe.

"It's going to be a nice fall day for your long ride," Ann volunteered pleasantly from the door. Ben stood at the edge of the piazza, back to her, shaping the brim of his black wool hat. The saddle horse tied at the post nickered softly.

"I'll be there soon as I'm ready," he called to her as though she could understand.

"See how the mist in the hollows look all pink faom the sun."

"I hadn't noticed," he said glumly.

"I wish I felt like going with you in the buggy. I've not been to the county seat since the first summer in Goodell."

"Wasn't that the day the vigilantes hung the horse thief?"

"Yes. And that spoiled the day for father and all of us."

"Well, this isn't going to be any pleasure trip for me, either."

"Do stop and get off every few miles—it will rest you. Twenty-five miles each way is a long ride when you're not used to it."

"Well, I might as well start. Likely there will be a lot of others on the road same as me. The draft notice said all men twenty to forty-five with names A to L come today for examination."

"When do you think you'll be back, Mr. Howe?"

"What difference does it make to you?" he snapped. "You got to stay here anyway account of Charley may come home any day. You'd ought to be glad I'm paying old Henry to do the chores. I got to go and get it over with. You know it ain't that I'm scared to go help put down the rebellion. It just don't seem necessary for them to need me, lame in this hip like I am. You know I get a hacking cough mighty easy."

"Yes, Mr. Howe, I know. We are both crippled, aren't we?"

Ben looked at her sharply.

Clapping on his hat, he strode hurriedly to the horse, mounted, and rode away without looking back.

Ann stood watching until he passed from sight across the flat toward town. Poor man—he is so worried about the draft—and Charley's running away, she thought. She shook her head sadly. Once you've loved a man it's second nature to keep on, whether he notices or not.

It was almost dark that night when Kate in the stable yard whinnied to her returning mate. Ann got up wearily from the edge of the piazza to stir up the fire in the cookstove.

Old Henry sauntered toward the stable. Ann heard his hail: "how'd you get along, Ben? Did they measure you for a uniform today?" Henry's cackle could be heard even above Ben's bitter answer.

She called to him pleasantly as he washed up at the bench outside—some trivial comment he would not have to answer. As he entered the kitchen she noticed his quick look around for sight of Charley's boots or battered straw hat. She knew he dreaded to ask if the runaway had returned.

He sat down heavily at the table and for a minute sat silent looking at nothing. Then with a gesture of casualness, he began, "I don't know how it will come out—about them calling me. The doctors say there's nothing the matter with me. They thumped me all over looked at my feet and my teeth. Old Doc Gordon, the one that came to town to help with the spotted fever, he was one of them."

"Did they ask about your family?" Ann asked hesitantly.

"I don't rightly remember, but I told them I farmed a lot."

Old Henry, entering, took up the conversation.

"See any of them copperheads being examined?" he asked knowingly.

"Might have been—I wouldn't know."

Ann asked, "Did you see a lot of Goodell men down there?"

"Yes, lots of them. Both your brothers, driving your father's rig.

And Will Harrison's oldest boy, horseback. Henry Laurie was there, drivin' that matched team of his to a top buggy."

Ben's dread of the draft put him into a frenzy of work, not only for himself, but to finding work for Ann to do as well. He pointed out that the wild plums were showering down onto the ground in the timber close to the Sugar Creek ford, and that she had better make plum sauce and plum butter while she was able. The garden Christina had tediously planted was yielding hordes of pickle material, vegetables to store, and sweet corn to cut and dry on cloth in the warm October sun.

There was very little money at the Howes that fall of '62, and that little was securely in Ben's keeping. When Ann told him she would need a few articles at the store even though there was no farm produce to trade, he said nothing. Entering Shute's store she asked old Anor to trust her for a pair of cotton flannel gloves for choring. Anor pulled at his chin whiskers and looked skeptical. Then he leaned forward, both hands on the counter. "I'm sorry, Miz Howe, but I've got to have my money today. For all I know, your man may not see fit to pay your bills."

"But Mr. Shute," she pleaded, "I have to have the gloves. Look at my hands. We will have wheat as soon as the machine comes and"—she swallowed hard and half-turned away—"we will have a fresh cow soon—and then I could bring butter."

"I'm sorry, Miz Howe, but I've been hearing things—about Ben—no offense, you understand."

Bitter tears welled up as Ann turned away from the counter and, with head held high, limped slowly toward the door. He had heard Mr. Howe was so angry with her he hadn't spoken a word to her in two weeks.

Alice, trotting along beside her, looked up and said, "Do you feel sick, Mama?"

"Yes, child, awful sick—at heart."

Chapter 24

"We're going to Lon Kelser's for Thanksgiving," Ben declared flatly.

Ann was more surprised at the abrupt breaking of his brooding silence than of the change in plans for the holiday. It had been almost three weeks since he had spoken a word in the house, save perhaps a mumbled answer to Alice's persistent questions—or to Charley.

Forgetting she really had no choice in the matter, Ann said rather disappointedly, "But Mr. Howe, I'd rather go to father's that day. The Kelsers are Baptists. I hardly know them."

"Lon comes from Massachusetts, too, though I never knew him till he came to town. I know his daughter that teaches. She was here with their preacher last harvest—remember?"

"Yes, I remember, though Miss Doskie stayed out in the field with you men while the minister's wife was here in the house. I was so tired from getting dinner for the harvesters I didn't enjoy having company."

"Well, we're going there Thursday."

"What could I take for dinner—some pies or a steamed pudding perhaps?"

Miss Doskie didn't say to bring anything. She knows you are poorly and can't hardly get your regular work done."

"I thought you said her father invited us."

"He did, but I was there by the school when it let out and Miss Doskie came out to give me the message."

"I see."

First Church held its traditional service on Thanksgiving at ten o'clock. Ben refused to attend but was willing enough to let Ann and

Alice off at the meetinghouse while he and Charley went on to Kelser's. He expected Stephen would bring the two of them along after the meeting.

Later, as Ann entered the strange house, she could hear Ben in the parlor entertaining the Kelsers with a detailed account of his long walk across Iowa in the spring of '54 looking for land. Mrs. Kelser excused herself for a moment to tend the dinner, leaving Ann to unwrap Alice. Ben was warming to his subject before an appreciative audience. He launched into a colorful account of buying the eighty acres and then building the sod cabin—single-handed—"So I could send for Charley and his mother."

Miss Kelser and her father were so interested in the account that they failed to notice Ann standing in the door.

Miss Kelser was asking incredulously, "And you mean that your first house was built of just sod?"

"That's right, and the floor was just hard-packed dirt that froze in winter and got muddy when it rained," Ben stated grandly.

"I cannot see how you stood it," the young woman said, shaking her head pityingly.

"Yes, it was pretty rugged for me that first winter," Ben admitted.

Although his back was turned Ann was sure he was smiling complacently. She interrupted sweetly with, "Yes, Miss Kelser, and if you ask, he will tell you how we lived in the cabin just as it was, for three years after I was married." She wanted these people to know the hardy pioneer Ben had not endured all those hardships alone.

Miss Kelser got up quickly to greet Ann and, after some gay chattering to the child, went to the kitchen.

Weary and discouraged, still puzzled at finding herself on this holiday in the house of strangers, Ann was glad to sit and wait for dinner to be called. Unmindful of the woman and the child, Ben and Lon Kelser set to probing each other's memories for recognition of mutual friends down east. The big plush covered family album had just been brought out when dinner was called.

Homeward-bound in the late afternoon, Ben resumed so deep a brooding silence that even Charley's questions could not penetrate.

A week passed before Ann had another chance to go to town. This time she could face old Anor Shute with head held high and not ask for credit. The cow had freshened as expected, and there was a little butter to trade.

It was pleasant to bargain around the store with the dollar and more the butter brought. First there were a few yards of flannel for Alice's nightgowns, then some new wide ribbons for her own old brown bonnet.

Totaling the goods, Anor allowed she had forty cents left to trade. "Now I want to see a pair of these feeting like my sister, Mrs. Peck, got here the wool ones," Ann said firmly. "I can knit the heel and toe and make a pair of socks for some soldier who maybe doesn't have any."

"They are thirty-seven cents," Anor allowed, "so that would make us about even."

Ann hesitated skeptically.

"Well, I guess I could throw in two—maybe three pieces of licorice for the boy and the girl, and one for old Ben himself," he cackled. Anor was always amiable when there was produce money to trade for merchandise.

"By the way, Miz Howe, has Ben heard any more about being drafted? I thought with you buying these things to make soldier socks, he'd got notice to go."

"He was examined—was all."

"They say enlistments ain't very lively, in the east especially. I figure the ones that's fit will go one way or other."

"But Mr. Shute, my husband is too old to go, and he isn't very well—he coughs a lot and gets down in the back awful easy seems like."

Anor cackled so loudly that others in the store turned to see.

"You tell him I said to be more careful a gettin' out of a warm bed in the middle of the night!"

Anor was still chuckling to himself as Ann gathered up her purchases and went out, blushing.

That evening, sitting in her low rocker by the heating stove, she got out the new knitting and began the tricky task of turning the heel on the ready-made tubelike sock. Ben sitting drowsily in his straight chair aroused himself enough to ask suspiciously, "What is that thing you are working on now?"

She did not look up from her work as she answered patiently, "They are called feeting—I guess because feet is all they lack of being a nice pair of socks for some soldier. I got the idea from Philo. Mrs. Goodell and most all the ladies in town are organizing a Soldiers' Relief Society to knit and sew for soldiers and their families."

"How much did those fool things cost?" he demanded.

"They were only thirty-seven cents," she said proudly.

"Well, of all the fool notions you ever had—bringing home more work to do when you can't get your own done!"

She kept her voice very low and calm as she went on, "Philo will send the socks to John so he can give them to whoever needs them in his company."

"Huh! Can't the gov'ment even clothe the army?"

She laughed lightly as she continued, still knitting, "Anor Shute thought you'd been called in the draft—me buying these feeting. He says there'll be a draft call in the spring."

"I can't see why you work for strangers when you can't get your own work done. The way you're going downhill lately, you'll be wanting me to move you to town."

"This isn't hard work, and I like to help with the relief work. Right now they are shipping barrels of beets and turnips and even carrots so the soldiers can have vegetables to keep them well."

"You mean the people are having to help the gov'ment feed 'em?"

"Oh they feed them, but not what they should get, especially in hospitals. I wonder if we could spare some turnips maybe."

"I say it ought to be enough if you finish that pair of those things."

"Wouldn't you like a pair of these nice wool socks, Mr. Howe?

"Who, me? I'm not a goin' to the army!"

He got up quickly, then hobbled toward the kitchen.

"Why, you are limping most as bad as I do," she said with sly solicitude, thinking he has acted older and stiff ever since he was examined for the draft.

When winter came shutting away the outside world of friends and family, Ann found new joy in the companionship of Alice. With each passing week the child seemed to become more of a person, a quiet mannerly child and a bit wistful at times as though sharing her mother's worries and discouragement. It was as if they shared an unspoken resentment of the dour Ben's rude neglect, and this drew mother and daughter closer together. Ann reveled in the child's responsive love.

From past experience, Ann knew better than to plan any observance of Christmas. Thus she could not be disappointed. On the eve of Christmas, when she went to tuck the child in her trundle bed in the cold room, she put a shawl around her own shoulders. Again she told the old story of the Star that paused over the stable half the world away from their snow-covered ridge. When she had finished she felt the retelling of the story had renewed her own faith.

At early breakfast the next morning, Ben turned half away from the table and sat stirring endlessly on his second cup of coffee. Finally he poured half into his saucer and, balancing it carefully, blew it cool and sipped noisily. At other meals with Charley and Alice chattering away, Ben's silence was less obvious.

When he had finished he arose quickly and, reaching for his boots and work frock, stepped to the door. The rising wind blew fresh snow across the floor and frosty air fogged the floor. Ann, watching, consoled herself it would be a bad day anyway. 'Perhaps I can go to dinner at the folks on New Year's,' she thought.

Within the week Ben changed and actually talked a little, not only to the children. At breakfast on New Years he asked if Ann wanted to go to Stephen's for dinner and did not seem surprised when she replied lightly, "I'm planning to go—anyway."

"Then I'll hitch Nellie to the sled."

"You're going, aren't you?"

"No."

"Charley can—"

"I'm keeping him here with me—we may go hunting."

At midmorning she saw him hitching the horse to the small sled and, hurrying to bundle Alice, was ready as he came leading the horse to the house.

With rare concern he held the horse till they were seated, then came to draw the shaggy old buffalo robe carefully around them. As she picked up the reins she said earnestly, "I do wish you were going."

"It's no place for me," he said shortly, turning away as he spoke. "Have a good time and make excuses for me."

She turned the horse past the stable as if to follow the ridge. He called after her, "You going around by Deacon Forbes?"

"Yes, I'm taking Lydia," she called back, "it will do her good to get away too."

For a full minute Ben stood watching the horse and sled bouncing along the old corn rows. As he turned to enter the stable, he muttered, "T'wouldn't be anyplace for me with Lydia still grievin' over Rollin and Philo tellin' about her John and the Fourth Cavalry down in Tennessee 'sleeping on the ground' she always says—well it ain't cold down there—I guess—and besides, he's a lot younger than me."

"I saw Bob Rose in town today," Ben announced at supper one evening late in March.

"How is Maria? I never get to see her any more."

"Tolerable, I guess. Old Bob says he is moving her and the hole kit-and-kaboodle of them out to Montana Territory."

"Poor Maria. I pity her having to go through all that, and at her age. She must be fifty. Why is he moving way out there?"

"A man has to look after hisself. Bob says it's getting' too settled up around here, and besides he says there's gold in most every little stream. Land is rich for farming, too. It's a far piece to travel in wagons, and they say the Sioux are on the rampage again, worst in years."

"Poor Maria!"

"It's Bob's lookout. He wants to sell his house in town, and I told him we'd look at it tomorrow. You can't stay here on the farm another year crippling around and hardly able to get a decent meal. I'm going to move you to town till you get over whatever ails you."

Ann spoke slowly and without show of emotion, realizing any eagerness of hers might turn Ben against the whole idea.

"I'll be ready tomorrow whenever you are, Mr. Howe."

The house proved to be a disappointment. It stood on low ground and, worst of all, had been built of green lumber, which had warped and shrunk, leaving great cracks that let in the wind even on such a mild day. Ann fairly held her breath lest Ben would buy it because old Bob asked only three hundred dollars.

After a long pause and much small talk, Ben said rather brusquely, "I ought to have a little better house—more comfortable for the family," he added lightly.

As they drove back toward the center of town, Ann remarked very casually, "Lydia Forbes said at New Year's dinner that Will is going to sell their house on Broad Street."

"You mean the one on the corner near your folks?"

"Yes," she replied simply, hoping her boldness in suggesting would not set Ben off on another tirade.

Instead he said gloomily, "Likely he'd want five, maybe six hundred for it, right on the stage road like it is."

"Lydia just said he wanted to sell it pretty bad, so he could save paying 12 percent interest on the farm."

Ann's hopes rose. If only Ben would buy the house. It was scarce a stone's throw from the Barretts. Then perhaps they could help just a little more.

The next day, after two hours of shrewd bargaining, the deal with Will Forbes was closed for four hundred and fifty dollars. Homeward bound, Ben grumbled long and loudly over being compelled to move to town anyway. And spending that much money all at once! And what a mess it was going to be, farming the place with poor hired help. The war was really taking all the men worth their salt! He ended with, "Now I hope you're satisfied," and slapped the reins down on Nellie's broad back.

Once the matter was decided, Ben was not one to dally. At midafternoon two days later the last pieces of furniture were being lashed to the top of the last wagon backed up to the piazza. Ann, with her wraps on, came to the door and stood for a minute watching, then turned back into the empty house. Perhaps it was the raucous cawing of crows overhead, or the plaintive call of mourning doves in the distance that stirred memory of another March day. She thought, I was younger then—and in love, coming out here atop the ox cart with all my things. Now I'm being hauled back to town in a buggy like some old woman.

She turned and walked through the echoing house, going from window to window as if to etch indelibly in memory the panorama of the rolling prairie hills. From the bedroom window the two graves inside the garden fence, sunken now, still held a thin remnant of old snow that lay like a soiled, disheveled coverlet over them. She thought bitterly—I wonder if he will bring me back here—beside them?

"Where are you?" Ben's querulous call rang through the echoing house. "Let's go—no use in moonin' around here in the cold."

She turned and followed him out the door, shutting it firmly behind her.

To Ann it seemed strange to be living right in the center of the townsite at the corner of Broad Street and the stage road. They were beginning to call it Fifth Avenue. At the farm the closest neighbor had been Lydia Forbes, a mile away. Here there was constant passing—settlers in covered wagons, adventurers bound for the Colorado gold fields, and huge swaying freighters.

Across the stage road, young Doctor Harbaugh occupied the

house Sam Cook had built and occupied until he got back into the army. The long cabin, quite uninhabitable, housed the blacksmith shop now run by only one of Debbie Hart's brothers, since the other had gone to Company E as a farrier. The town bell that had stood close by now rested on the roof of what had been the first schoolhouse, and which now housed the fire brigade equipment.

First church, a block down the street and facing Mr. Goodell's park, had grown with the town and could seat almost the whole town. With its ells and additions it resembled a cathedral, a prairie cathedral of wood, built in the shape of a cross. The first families had stayed pretty loyal, although some had gone to join the Baptists and the Methodists who still met in homes on a Sabbath.

Directly opposite First Church a small wooden building housed Mike Sydon's private bank. Henry Laurie was cashier and bookkeeper, and on occasion was seen sweeping out the place and carrying in fuel. Henry was on his way to becoming a solid citizen. He drove a matched team of bays to a top buggy when taking Postmaster Spensley's daughter for a ride evenings.

Henry had taken charge of the drilling when Sam Cook went into the army. After Company E, Fourth Cavalry, had been mustered into the service, things had quieted down for a time. Later, when there were threats of rebel raids up from Missouri, Mike Sydon had quietly promoted formation of the Home Guards. Few people knew then that Mike was in with J. B. Goodell on building and filling the wool warehouse down beyond the railroad grade. Henry's affability outweighed the prejudice against all bankers, and he had been elected captain of the Guards.

Anor Shute's new store occupied a frame building between J. Coker's harness shop and the bank. Unlike its neighbors, it needed no false front, for it was actually two stories high, with an outside stairway that led to living quarters above. A wide wooden awning extended over a platform that reached out almost to the hitching rack in front.

On Amelia Hanlon's first visit, Ann learned many of the less-known goings-on in town. Amelia practically wept when she related how the new Soolders' Relief, under Julia Goodell's able management, had attracted all the capable needle workers in town. As a result, The Ladies' Benevolent Society of First Church was practically extinct. And they had faithfully looked after the poor of the town ever since '55.

Later, when Ann asked about Gerty Buderfa, Amelia glanced about as though expecting eavesdroppers. "It's no wonder Gerty feels like an outsider," Amelia declared, "the only woman in town with a husband in the rebel army. Where else would he have gone right after Fort Sulmter!"

"Do you suppose she hears from him?" Ann asked.

Amelia shrugged her shoulders.

"We tried to find out from Mr. Spensley, but he wouldn't tell us a thing. The idea of him being so close-mouthed about the mail!"

"Poor woman, she must be having a hard time with Jim gone these two years," Ann said sympathetically. "Likely she needs help from the Benevolent Ladies right along."

"She will have to do the best she can," Amelia said firmly, "because we aren't about to help a rebel family, even if they do need it! Besides, her Jimmie is working at Clack's mill same as his father did."

"But Amelia, what if Jim didn't go south? They say he was the one that put Sam Woodburn in the notion of going west years ago."

Amelia shrugged her shoulders.

"I expect you've heard about Julia Goodell giving up her parlor for the relief work," she continued. "She said she never used it now Mr. Goodell is in Washington City practically all the time. Poor dear, she doesn't have time to be lonesome. Did you hear about all the cotton she got?"

"Why no, I've not heard any of these things. This town needs a newspaper, doesn't it?"

"They dropped a whole big bale of cotton on Julia's doorstep, to make comforters for the relief—a whole bale! Lol Phipps told the men there were only ten bales alloted to the whole state!"

"Father always said J. B. knew the right people," Ann said.

If Ann had expected an easier life in town, with more rest and quiet, she was doomed to disappointment. The muddy roads and streets had scarcely begun to dry when the procession of visitors and callers began. Town women bound to or from the stores stopped by. Farm women waiting while husbands were at the mill or the blacksmith shop stopped by, preferably at dinnertime, knowing Ann would put an extra plate on the table.

A young Negro woman, seeking family washings to do, stopped the day after Amelia's visit. For several days Ann postponed asking

Ben's permission to hire the woman for fifty cents each washing. She feared his objection for such extravagance. Later, when she brought up the subject, he said he didn't see any reason why she couldn't do the washings. Other women did.

"But Mr. Howe," she explained patiently, "by the time I draw all the water and get it on to heat I am so tired I can scarce stand."

"I suppose I'll have to put in a pump. I'll be needing one."

Ann had scarcely gotten the house in order after the moving when Ben got the urge to plant garden. "That little patch here in the back yard is too small," he declared, "so we'll plant most of it at the farm. Jake's got the garden out there plowed and ready. I'm not about to be buying garden truck to eat!"

Riding along silently in the open buggy, the raw chill of the April morning made her cough violently. As she pulled her shawl closer about her shoulders, Ben eyed her disapprovingly. "Don't seem like you can stand much anymore. Always coughing your head off and limping around. I figured if I moved you to town you'd get rested and snap out of whatever ails you. It looks like I should a brought Charley to help me with the planting."

"Yes, Mr. Howe, I do cough and I do limp, but I'll help you as long as I'm able."

After a bit he said rather off-handedly, "I told Charley not to go near the railroad gang today—they must be six miles or more east of town."

"If he takes a notion he will go, knowing we are gone for the day."

Ben looked at her sharply, amazed at her frankness, then conceded grudgingly, "Might be so, but anyway he'll be back in time to get the cow in time to milk. He is pretty dependable that way."

As they entered the garden at the farm, mellow and black from the plowing, Ben stopped stock still, letting the implements fall to the ground with a clatter. The weathered marker board at Laura's grave lay broken in the grass still bearing the dirty hoof print of the trampling plow horse.

Angrily Ben turned and yelled, "Jake—you fool, come here!"

There was no answer.

He hurried forward and, picking up the fragments, stood fitting them together. Ann came and touched his elbow, and her voice full of understanding. "Wouldn't you like to move the two of them to the new cemetery? You know they've put up a fence so the town cattle can never trample on it."

"No," he barked. "I want them to stay here—I'll not be living in town always."

He stooped and carefully fitted the broken pieces of the board together on the end of the grave.

As he straightened up he said gruffly, "This kind of thing just goes to show what trouble movin' you to town is making me—and it isn't over."

He picked up the tools and faced her.

"What can you do best—hoe the trenches, or drop the seeds?"

"I think I can hoe out the trenches easier."

She took the hoe from him and began the trench for peas. Perhaps she wavered a bit on her feet in the soft earth, for Ben, watching her, barked, "You've got to get started straight!"

Get started straight—get started straight! she thought. I didn't get started straight seven years ago—I was meek when I should have been strong.

Chapter 25

"Father sent over a batch of Iowa City papers for you," Ann said as she began gathering the supper dishes. Ben poured his coffee into the saucer and sipped it noisily.

Without looking up he said very casually, "Anything about the draft or about a man hirin' a substitute?"

"I haven't read them, but Father would know. You'd think he was going to be drafted or something, in the way he frets and talks about it. He says the government is going to announce something important about it July first." She smiled happily as she added, "But we won't have to worry about you for now, will we?"

"I always said I was too old for this soldiering," he said complacently.

"Bud Buderfa told us when we were after the cows that his brother Jimmie is going to hire out as a substitute because his mother needs the money," Charley said, adding in amazement, "he said the bounty will be three hundred dollars!"

"Do you think the Home Guards can get along without your brother Emery while he goes in the draft?" Ben said with a sneer. "You must know about him being on the list over in the provost marshal's office — being over at your folks so much like you are."

"I didn't know," Ann murmured rather helplessly. Then, recovering from the surprise, she said defensively, "But Mr. Howe, the Home Guards are needed, like if there'd be a raid up from Missouri — or there was trouble with rebel sympathizers."

"There ain't either one likely. Though," he conceded, "nobody ever thought General Lee would strike north toward Pennsylvania like he is doing."

He sipped at his coffee again. "Three hundred dollars! That's a heap of money. I can't see how Emery would raise that much — that is, if he is bound to stay with the Home Guards. Now take a young feller like Jimmie Buderfa, he can take that bounty money and help his mother out of a bad fix—that and the thirteen a month he'd draw as a soldier."

"Poor Gerty," Ann sighed, turning away, "she has trouble enough with her man gone these two years, and now her boy near grown up to go. What if the two would meet in battle, say!"

"That would be a pretty kettle of fish, I'd say!"

Ann was now washing dishes at the other table. She turned to say, "Father thinks the steam cars will run into town by the Fourth of July. Won't that be nice?"

"I don't know. Haven't been out to see where they are. I can't understand why folks get so excited over the railroad coming—and even going out to see a gang of jabbering Irish lay rails on ties!"

"They are working in that forty acres of Aunt Philo's east of town," Charley volunteered eagerly.

"How come you know so well where they are, when I've told you not to go near?" his father asked sharply.

"One of the boys told me."

Still trying to keep the conversation going pleasantly, Ann said, "I wonder if Mr. Goodell will come home from Congress for the railroad celebration on the Fourth."

"Huh! He wouldn't miss it! Likely he has a pass on the M & M and all the other lines clear from Washington City. The railroads know which side their bread is buttered on, as they say."

"I heard the town is planning a big celebration with a picnic in Hanlon's grove after the train comes in. I am so anxious for Alice to see the steam cars come to town for the first time. Wouldn't you like to go , Mr. Howe?"

"Huh! Done up as you are," he growled, "I don't see how you can get down to the track, even if they do get to town. Don't count on me takin' you. I got to go to the farm."

"I'll manage somehow. Alice would be disappointed and I'd not think of letting her go down even to the meetinghouse corner with all that crowd in town. They say folks are coming from miles around— even from way over in Jason County."

"Alice could see the cars all the rest of her life—they aren't much to see."

"My folks will be going, and I thought we could put our dinner with theirs and Philo's and have a nice—time—"

"Listenin' to a lot of dry speeches and then eat a cold dinner sitting on the ground. No! I've got two men hewin' out in the frame for my new barn. You'd better get your own work done and then maybe rest instead of galavantin' around to celebrations."

He set down his coffee cup, pulled back his chair, and got up hastily. Charley looked smugly across at Ann as though saying that the old man told her off that time!

It was better for her not to notice the boy's glances.

As Ben stood by the sitting room table lighting the kerosene lamp, Alice ran to the stand, fascinated watching the yellow flame spread across the wick. Ann called to Ben, "Aren't we all thankful for the nice new lamp? It gives a lot more light than candles, doesn't it?"

"I guess so," he said grudgingly, "but I didn't know it would take so much kerosene at fifty cents a gallon."

Ben had bought the lamp two weeks before, following a spell of moody silence that lasted five days. At the first fuel refilling he laid the blame on Dave Myers at Harve Blue's store for selling him a contraption that took so much to keep it going.

A faint glow in the east warned Ann, wakeful in the closeness of the small bedroom, that it was time to be up if she was to get full enjoyment of the holiday. She eased out of bed and began dressing, fearful lest she waken Ben. If I get my work done while it's cool and before he gets up, maybe he won't be so upset if I go to see the cars come to town—and the picnic, too, she was thinking.

As she began sweeping the kitchen, a shadowy figure crept close past the window. In an instant she heard Charley's feet hit the floor in the room above. She smiled, knowing well that Charley had left a string tied to his toe and the end dangling out the window for some boy to waken him. A moment later the shingles on the porch creaked and then the slight sound of Charley sliding over the edge and the muffled thud of his bare feet. Minutes later, the town bell on the shanty across the street began ringing jerkily. So that was where he went in such a hurry.

Ann resumed her sweeping and, having finished, brought water from the well to scrub the front piazza. Across the street old Mr. Southlin stood outside clad in his long nightshirt demanding quiet at such an unearthly hour, and getting only snickers from the culprits perched on the roof beside the bell. Ann stepped back quickly lest she embarrass the old gentleman.

At the usual time Ann put on meat and potatoes to fry. When the fragrance of the coffee wakened Ben, he came out hurriedly and went to the stable to milk. Nonchalantly, Charley appeared from nowhere and went to wait for his father to turn out the cow for him to take to graze beyond the town. If Ben suspected the boy's part in the early bell ringing, he at least said nothing.

At midmorning, after waiting in vain for Stephen to stop with the buggy, Ann took Alice by the hand and started slowly down the board walk toward the track, carrying a parasol.

From all directions townfolks and visitors were converging on the bare little depot that M & M had hastily erected where the new track skirted Goodell's park. The few remaining members of the brass band, now discharged and wearing such parts of their gray uniforms as still lasted, hurried along tootling playfully, much to the enjoyment of small boys following them.

Beyond Mike Sydon's private bank, Ann followed the dusty path past Sarah Phipp's and the flagpole opposite. The park with its scattering of spindling maple trees was already occupied by a score or more of farm wagons and a few buggies whose drivers had tethered their horses to graze or left them munching grain and a wisp of hay from the backs of vehicles. Beneath the wagons, mongrel farm dogs lay panting in the shade, eyeing each other suspiciously.

Ann and Alice walked slower and slower as they approached the depot where the crowd was gathering around a huge welcome sign built across the tracks and covered with fresh green boughs brought clear from Jardine's timber. Wide white boards bore the lettering, "Goodell, the Gateway to the West Welcomes the M & M."

The crowd grew impatient waiting in the sun, after the advertised time of arrival of the train had passed. Ann stood wearily, holding Alice by the hand, especially when the child sighted Charley jostling among the boys atop some freight cars, and had to be restrained. Only the arrival of Phil hurrying across the park kept the child from tears.

"I was afraid you couldn't come for having to get dinner for your boarders," Ann managed to say.

"This is Independence Day and I'm being independent," the younger woman said, "so I told them at breakfast to line up at the picnic at Hanlon's grove and there would be plenty to eat. I see father sitting in the buggy over there on the other side."

"I'm going over there and sit down to wait," Ann said wearily.

"You hadn't better go just yet. Father is talking business with Jimmie Buderfa and I guess you know what about. It will all come out soon enough. Did Old I-c-e-b-e-r-g g-o to the f-a-r-m today?"

Ann nodded and smiled at Alice's puzzled look about the spelling. She was puzzling over her father talking business with Gerty's boy.

When the train was at last sighted, the brass blared its best. By the time the gaily painted Anton LeClaire came puffing up the slope with its four-car train, it was completing the third rendition of the "Star-Spangled Banner."

Cautiously the engine, showering wood sparks, slowed to push its way through the cheering crowd, and came to a stop with the last car directly beneath the welcome arch. As the train stopped, Postmaster Spensley was hustled through the crowd and climbed aboard to greet the score or more of railroad officials and important citizens from towns along the line, who came pouring across the couplers from the two coaches decked with bunting. Citizen Spensley, although dressed in his Sabbath-best suit and wearing a low-crowned black hat, appeared a little frowsy among the dignitaries he was to welcome. Most of them wore long-tailed coats and high silk hats.

Meanwhile Ray Clarkson the local photographer hurried to set up his equipment at the far end of the flat car platform and then hastened forward to plead with Spensley and the first M & M official to hold perfectly still while he ducked beneath the black cloth and began counting time with upraised hand.

During all this, the lesser citizens on the trains had been detained in the last coach. But the people wanted none of them anyway. "We want J. B. Goodell! We want J. B.!" the crowd chanted.

"Now I think that's real nice," Philo said innocently, "having folks call for him even if he couldn't come clear from Washington City. Won't Julia be proud! Goodness knows, he didn't build the railroad, but at least he kept after them till they did."

A bearded young settler standing nearby assured her, "Lady, don't worry none. He's there and waiting to make a big show."

Mr. Spensley welcomed the visiting delegation briefly and withdrew in favor of some tall-hatted stranger. The clamor of the crowd increased. With difficulty the city man made himself heard as he hastily concluded, "And now I give you the chairman and first speaker on this great day in the history of your little city—your friend and my friend—the aggressive pioneer—the patriot—the champion of the people! The Honorable J. B. Goodell!"

The crowd cheered wildly as the familiar short, stout figure appeared in the door of the last coach. Stepping to the railing, he paused dramatically silent for a moment and dabbed at a tear with his handkerchief. Slowly he removed his tall hat and laid it carefully beside him, took out his gold watch, and noted the time.

The settler nearby half-turned away as though in disgust. "Likely the old gent'll make that damned recruitin' speech again!"

"Distinguished guests, citizens of this fair city, and fellow Republicans—" he began grandly.

"We ain't all Republicans," the same settler shouted back, "not by a jugful!"

"He acts like he'd sampled his own jug," Philo whispered.

J. B. Goodell was launched into a lengthy account of the years of misfortune the M & M had suffered, and his own role in bringing the rialroad to completion. He was praising the foresight of Powhatan County people for subscribing enough railroad bonds to complete the line, when a young fellow came out of the telegraph office waving a yellow dispatch. He wormed his way into the crowd, and moments later Goodell stopped speaking and reached down for the paper. The crowd stirred uneasily. Telegrams always brought bad news.

Goodell read hastily, then, smiling broadly, waved the telegrams as he shouted, "I have good news for all loyal citizens— Vicksburg has just surrendered—and today Lee is retreating south from Gettysburg, Pennsylvania, after Pickett's charge was repulsed yesterday!"

The crowd went wild with joy. It was some time before they regained any interest in the railroad celebration, the Fourth of July, or J. B. Goodell's elaborate patriotic speech. Many drifted away from the train to gather in knots to discuss the news, for there was scarcely a family in town or surrounding country who did not have kin with Company E, Fourth Cavalry, before Vicksburg.

The settler who had been standing near Ann and Philo hurried to untie his saddle horse, mounted and rode around the crowd, shouting and waving his battered hat. As his horse hurdled the tracks, he shouted, "Hurrah for Jeff Davis!" and was gone down the Blue Knob road.

The Honorable Goodell was too intent on holding the attention of the crowd to notice the fracas. He was trying to make these people see this great day as he saw it—the day he had planned and worked for, ever since that raw March day in '54 when firse he set foot on that barren ridge — the day his town would have a railroad!

Then, methodically he went through the usual patriotic phrases, the ones he had used so often since Fort Sumter — uphold Mr. Lincoln — save the Union. He was mentally checking them off as spoken, like beads on a cord — the sanctity of the Constitution — our heritage from the Founding Fathers. As his voice went on, his thoughts rambled. I should have mentioned Homer. Hanlon and Tom Holt — who else helped stake out the townsite — oh, yes, young Laurie — they helped start the colony, but they named it for me — I planned it that way — the depot a stone's throw from my house — but the switch tracks, I must speak to Byington to move them farther away — toward Lol Phipp's place.

The trite phrases were soon pretty well used up, and he must devote full attention to making a strong finish. Enlistments — that was the key to a successful conclusion. He began to bear down heavily on any within the sound of his voice who delayed volunteering. "Why, even the older men — men with gray beards — are forming a company over in Jason County. Every man regardless of age can do something to save the Union," he thundered.

Philo confided to Ann, "When I hear band music or a thrilling speech like this, I get all tingly!"

"I guess I am too tired to notice," Ann said wearily.

"Hannah is going to weep if Emery insists on going right home after the speaking and miss the parade and picnic."

"Oh, that would be too bad — to ride five miles to town in a wagon and miss all that. But why?" Ann asked.

"I imagine Emery will feel funny about being seen around here wondering what folks are going to say when it all comes out."

"What comes out?"

"That father is hiring a substitute for him in the draft!" Philo whispered. For what else do you think father was talking so earnestly with Jimmie Buderfa just now?

"I never thought of that," Ann whispered back.

At the close of the speech, the brass band led the parade to Hanlon's grove. By clever fist work, Charley won the honor of carrying the front of the big drum. They were followed by several wagons decorated with bunting and bearing the distinguished visitors, who had difficulty keeping on their tall hats when the wagons bounced over the ruts on Main Street.

Behind came all manner of vehicles, including the familiar big old freighter of Will Sheridan's, pulled this time by six horses instead of oxen. Some who watched the parade remarked that so many good horses together made a pretty valuable team—with cavalry horses worth a hundred-twenty apiece.

After the crowd left, Lol Phipps's wagon backed up to the baggage car to take two hogheads containing ice cream made only yesterday at Davenport—the special treat of the M & M Railroad for the celebration. Goodell had advised his friend Byington to provide this, instead of the hard cider or even liquor other towns had received on like occasions.

In the sparse shade of Homer Hanlon's locust grove, the long tables had been set up, upon which each housewife proudly set her culinary masterpiece. The combined effect was staggering to behold. With difficulty the young were restrained from the feast, and a few instructed husbands, too, had to be shooed away from the tables until Reverend Heath's blessing.

At once Eli Henderson, the newly arrived provost marshal, and Postmaster Spensley sought out Congressman Goodell and held an earnest conference. Eli, the stranger, whose very title sounded ominously mysterious, appeared to be upset over something. Goodell, with sharp forceful gestures and a ready flow of words, with an occasional pat on the back, appeared to be bolstering this emissary of the federal government. Poor Julia Goodell, who had scarcely had a word with her husband all day, finally gave up and led her children to the tables and filled their plates.

Lol Phipps and Reverend Heath, waiting impatiently for the three to finish their conference, kept glancing restlessly at the rapidly disappearing food supply. Finally Phipps, who felt no hero worship toward his fellow townsman, interrupted with, "Now, J. B., Reverend Heath here thinks we should follow up these Union victories with a special prayer service of thankfulness. We thought though we'd better ask you, and if you agreed we could announce it right here. It might help enlistments, too."

"Fine idea, Lol," the congressman rumbled. "Fine! Mr. Lincoln was saying to me just the other day—"

To think that a fellow townsman had gone so far as to be a close friend of Abe Lincoln!

After the feast had been consumed, the hogsheads were opened and the ladeling of ice cream began. It was a trifle soft, but what could you expect after being shipped clear from Davenport "by rail," as the new expression was? Old timers, waiting, spoke of how it used to take them four days, maybe five to freight through from the river—and "Look how times have changed since '54."

Stephen Barrett attended the picnic with some misgivings, rather than disappoint his family. Folks were already probably talking about his hiring a substitute for Emery—and the substitute the son of a rebel at that. Perhaps, he thought, Emery should have waited for the draft—three hundred dollars—a fortune to spend on only one of them—there was still Stan coming along—and even Ben Howe. He couldn't buy them all off—and what would Philo think of the others not going, with her John already a volunteer?

No one had much real reason to tarry longer at the grove. Settlers who had come miles in wagons were anxious to start home for chores. The railroad officials consulted their gold watches frequently and talked of getting back to Iowa City in time for supper at the Hawkeye House. They were even more restless after hearing spasmodic blasts from the Anton LeClaire's whistle. Ann wondered idly if Ben would hear the whistle and if Charley would be bold enough to brag of the part in the escapade she was sure he had taken.

Chapter 26

"I don't believe you've lifted a hand since I went to the farm this morning, "Ben stormed at her as he stood washing for supper three days after the celebration. "And for the life of me I can't see what you are coming to—laying in bed when you've got work to do!"

Ann, at the cookstove swayed on her feet as she turned toward him, speaking carefully as though explaining to a child, "I'm sick, Mr. Howe, and what little I did today I leaned on a chair, I'm so weak and dizzy from coughing."

"You went to the celebrarion Saturday," he accused.

"I wanted Alice to see the steam cars come to town."

He was eyeing her closely as he wiped on the roller towel. "Seems like you look pretty peaked for a woman not doing a thing outside of a little housekeeping. Must be you don't weigh a hundred."

"No, Mr. Howe, and even Brooks Brothers Elixir hasn't helped me."

"You mean you've been spending my money for that sort of patent medicine? You ought to try old Mrs. Norton's mixture. 'Twon't cost hardly anything. Ezra says she was good after she took it a spell."

"I'll try to get the recipe from her, maybe tomorrow afternoon at the prayer meeting."

"How's that? Prayer meetin' in the afternoon?"

"It is a meeting to give thanks for the success of our armies and pray for those in service, Mr. Howe. Philo wants me to go with her— she is so worried and upset after every big battle when she is sure John might have been in it—like Vicksburg, now."

Charley piped up with, "Jimmie Buderfa says he hopes they send him down there—he wants to join Company E. He is going as a substitute, but he wouldn't tell us who for. We tried to pump him when we were driving in the cows." After a moment the boy continued wonderingly, "He seems awful young to be a soldier, someway."

Folks flocked to First Church that Thursday afternoon until there was only standing room. The tie racks along both streets were full of teams hitched to farm wagons and buggies. By the time the service began the stores were deserted and Anor Shute even closed up.

Stephen Barrett had gone early to sit thoughtfully in his own pew where Ann and Philo joined him. The regular members of the church were there in force—Julia Goodell, the Hanlons, the Holts, the Forbes, and the Phipps. Strangers were urged to come right in and sit in private pews.

Gerty Buderfa entered and stood at the door for a moment as though looking for a seat. With head held high, she walked down the center aisle and paused questioningly beside the Barrett pew. Ann leaned over and touched her arm, saying, "Do come sit with us." It was good of you to come," unmindful of the stares and murmurs.

"I belong here same as you do, Miz Howe, though most folks don't believe it."

"Yes, of course you do, with Jimmie going so soon, I hear."

"T'ain't only that, Miss Howe. Folks never gave me a chance after Jim left. I'd of helped with the sewing and bandages and quilts if they'd thought I was good enough. Now Jim's gone—I guess you've heard—I got word from his pard—killed in a rock slide in Colorado."

"Oh, Gerty, I never knew," Ann murmured simply, thinking—and there folks believed she was a copperhead.

The service began with Reverend Heath presiding, assisted by the Baptist minister Branson, who led off the prayer service. After his, a dozen or more prayers followed. Folks just rose and in their own words thanked the Lord for the Union victories and pleaded for the safe return of those who still fought on. Others prayed for peace and victory, particularly those with more boys growing up. Tom Holt's wife prayed for "our fallen heroes who lie buried on foreign soil." At this Lydia Forbes suppressed a moan. Her Rollin lay somewhere in Tennessee.

Stephen Barrett did not rise to pray as was his custom, even though he felt Reverend Heath's stern gaze rest questioningly upon him. He had been reluctant to attend, but feared his absence would be more noticeable. He had been baffled and uncertain of his own judgment every since hiring Jimmie Buderfa as a substitute. Perhaps Emery should have enlisted. Folks would likely remember and question that for a long time to come.

Just before the close, Reverend Heath asked for announcements. Julia Goodell arose to report, "The Soldier's Relief will hold a benefit festival in that empty storeroom on Main Street tomorrow evening in honor of those who are due to leave for the army in August. An admission of twenty-five cents will be collected, or that value in vegetables such as will stand shipping to our army hospitals. All cash will be kept here in town to help families of our heroes in the service."

At Mrs. Goodell's request, Postmaster Spensley then arose to read the list of names, copies, so he said, from the provost marshal's office. The old gentlemen stumbled over the second name, so that it came out as "Em—I mean—er—James W. Buderfa."

Stephen Barrett stirred uncomfortably.

Mr. Spensley droned on, stopping impressively after each name until he came to "Henry Ford of Pleasant View Township." Although the names were no surprise, it brought a murmur of comment and some people turned around to see how Eli Henderson, the provost, would react to those Blue Knob names on his list. Eli lounged against the wall near the door.

After the benediction, Stephen Barrett slipped away before the ladies came past to shake hands with Philo and Ann. Gerty Buderfa held her ground and accepted their greetings as though she had not been an outcast for two years.

The next evening at dusk, the sound of the brass band roused Ben from his reading. "Now what are they up to?" he called. "Isn't that the same old 'Listen to the Mocking Bird' piece?"

"Yes, Mr. Howe, and isn't it pretty? You can even hear the drum sticks tapping in the rims in the chorus."

She went on to explain the purpose of the festival, adding a bit too proudly that it was all for Soldiers' Relief.

"I hope you didn't work making a lot of those fool caps like your lady friends fitted out E Company with—a crossbreed between a sunbonnet and a women's nightcap, if I ever saw one."

"No, Mr. Howe, I didn't make any havelocks for the men either then or now." She was tempted to remind him that he had kept her at home boiling sorghum the afternoon John's company left town. She hoped he would not ask her if she furnished anything for the evening's festival. Her molasses cookies had been safely out of the house an hour before he came from the farm.

Later, when the sound of the fiddle and the high-pitched droning voice of the caller could be heard, Ben laid down his paper in disgust. "What is this town coming to—having dances?"

"It's wartime, Mr. Howe—and folks do things different. They're just singing games and not real dancing."

"I hear they're lettin' a lot of Iowa men come home on veteran furloughs," he complained. "I suppose John will be honeying up to your sister, making up for lost time. Is she at the festival, as you call it, tonight?"

"She was going to help in the refreshment booth."

"It's a poor place for a woman with no husband along!"

"But she will be with Julia Goodell and Sarah and the others."

"Well, she is the same as a widow, ain't she? Her man ain't been home for more'n a year. Widows need watchin'—they get pretty hot."

"She misses him," Ann said indignantly, "just like I miss you being gone day after day like you are, Mr. Howe."

"When I'm gone there's plenty you could be doing around here. What's all those little pieces you're fiddlin' with there?"

"I'm starting a quilt for Alice."

"Huh! It don't seem like she'll be needin' it for her settin' out very soon!"

"It isn't that she needs it, but sometimes I get to feeling I have so much to do and so little time to do it all." She sighed wearily.

He looked at her sharply. What fool notion has she got now?

"'Twould seem you'd be better to put up cucumber pickles and green tomato relish and such things—and maybe some apple butter—and you could put out apples to dry for winter 'stead of working on a quilt!"

"I will try to make apple butter if you'll bring me the apples. You know you didn't like wild crabapple butter, remember?"

"A fellow was tellin' me about a good apple orchard up near the LeGrand mill—set out before his town was even started—widow woman has it—her man died of spotted fever last year. There ain't any decent apples any closer. Them on that pizzlin' tree your brother lugged out from the East are gnarley—no taste."

Ann busy with the quilt pieces thought, I'll never ask him to bring me any apples from a widow woman's orchard—if we never have apple butter.

Chapter 27

"Wheat went up like I said it would when Grant opened up the Mississippi," Ben said triumphantly at breakfast one morning in mid-November. He shoved his chair back from the table as he said, "It's going to bring me seventy-five cents a bushel, and I'll be shoveling it into a freight car here in town stead of hauling to Iowa City or even Brooksville.

Ann looked up in surprise at Ben's apparent joviality and said, "Then you'll be home for dinner with Alice and me."

At once his manner changed. "You might know it'll take two wagonloads to haul a hundred bushels. No! I'll be going right back for the second load. I'll eat with Jake at the farm."

"Wouldn't you rather eat a good dinner here with us?"

"No, I'm in a hurry to get the hundred delivered and put another loan on the wagon to take to mill at LeGrand early tomorrow."

"But Mr. Howe, I'd think you would bring it to Captain Clack's mill right here in town—most everybody uses his flour."

"No! I'd not feather his nest by patronizing him."

"But it's twenty miles to LeGrand."

"I tell you I want to go up there."

"Why don't you let Jake make the trip for you?" she persisted. "You pay him—and besides, it's going to get colder. I've seen a lot of ducks going south."

"'Tain't any farther in bad weather than in good."

"Tomorrow is Friday and quite likely you'd have to wait your turn at the mill, and then you wouldn't get home before the Sabbath."

"I'm going anyway."

She turned away defeated and began stacking the dishes. Ben

was still leaning forward in his chair as though thinking, and a little reluctant to leave after all.

She glanced toward him and thought—once before I questioned his being so much at the timber and all the time he was getting out saw logs for rebuilding our house as a surprise to me—I shouldn't expect to know what he is doing I guess.

Ben finally rose from the table and began pulling on his boots. She hurried to the closet and returned as he was opening the kitchen door. "Here, Mr. Howe, you must take this heavy muffler I knit for you years ago. When it turns cold you'll be glad you have it."

He looked at her skeptically and swung it around his neck as he went out wordlessly.

Ann watched him from the window as he led the horse from the stable and rode away toward the farm to get the wagon. It was a dull frosty morning, gray and dismal—a good day to work on the quilt here by the fire.

When Philo stopped by later that morning, she found her delving into the scrap bag and cutting pieces. As the younger woman slipped out of her shawl she said gaily, "I see you have started your winter evening pick up work." It was a relief to find Ann up and about the house. So often of late she found her in bed racked with coughing, and Alice playing quietly nearby. Today her face was flushed instead of the usual pallor.

"Who is this quilt for?" she asked. "I thought you had plenty."

"It's for me," Alice lisped proudly.

"Well, little Miss, you won't be needing one for your setting out anytime soon," Philo teased.

"It's just that I want to get as much done as I can."

"It's going to get colder according to Mrs. Southlin,"—Philo hastily changed the subject—"because she stopped me just now to say her rheumatism is worse—and that is a sure sign."

"Yes, I tried to tell Mr. Howe he had better wait till it cleared, but he would go to mill tomorrow. He is staying at the farm to get an early start—for LeGrand. He was in a hurry to get the first load and said he'd simply have to get down to Amos Long's to get the sole of his boot pegged down again, in case he has to walk to keep warm on the road."

"That poor woman is having a hard time to support the family—Amos isn't at all well—he tried to cobble a little. I hear she makes men's suits and besides that, since the railroad ends here she has been sewing up wagon covers for settlers outfitting to go west. She has a sewing maching, I'd have you know."

At four Charley came from school and, finding his father would not be home to milk, went directly to get the cow from the herd on the prairie. Surprisingly, he seemed to feel some responsibility and even brought in wood without being asked.

Later, occupying his father's chair in the sitting room, he asked, "Aunt Ann, where does father stay when he goes to mill?"

"He is staying at Jake's tonight, so he can start early," she replied, trying to be casual.

"But where does he stay while he waits at the mill?"

"He stays at a tavern in LeGrand, of course. Why?"

"Oh, nothing."

The weather did turn bad. Mrs. Southlin's rheumatism had been correct. Saturday was cold, and the wind whipping around the house drove in the damp chill. Ann sat by the stove intent on the quilt top that seemed to grow too slowly. She tried not to wonder where Ben was or what he was doing. At early suppertime, waiting for Charley to bring in the milk, she stood watching the sun set pale yellow beneath gray clouds that crowded ominously upon it. Snow began falling early.

It was almost bed time Monday evening when Ben arrived from the mill. She heard the rumble of the wagon on the frozen street and sent Charley to the stable with the lantern. In a few minutes Ben came in, stamping the snow from his boots, as casual as though he had been to the store.

"What sort of trip did you have?" she asked cheerily, as she went about putting on a late supper for him.

"Fair to middlin'. I guess you know it stormed, but I got the flour in the wagon covered with canvas. It will be all right till morning."

"You must have had to wait a long time at the mill," she observed.

"The river was low. Been dry all fall. They had to wait for the dam to fill every few hours. That was what held me up."

He did not look up, but sat carefully examining the sole of his right boot.

"That was too bad, your having to wait your turn so long. Where did you stay?"

"Widow woman's place, where I always stay."

"Aunt Ann said you stayed at the tavern," Charley said as though disappointed.

"She has that real nice apple orchard I told you about—guess her man must 've set it out in '51 or '52. That country was settled before this town was."

Ben continued examining his boot and the sore spot on his foot, until his supper was ready.

"Guess I'll have to wear my old pair tomorrow. I'll try Amos Long once more and see if he can peg this sole so it will stay."

"Did you bring the bran and mill feed for our cow, or did you let the miller have it on his bill?"

"You act terrible interested in my business. I gave the mill feed to the widow woman. I stopped on the way home and put the sacks in the shed. Her cow needed the feed, and her trying to make a little money sellin' milk at five cents a quart. Mind you, there's a hard-working woman. She gets things done!"

"Did the mill run on the Sabbath?" she asked, still probing.

"Can't say. I set by the fire all day."

Ben shoved his chair up to the table and began eating silently. When he was nearly finished he said, "I have to go to Evan's mine after coal tomorrow."

"I was in hopes you'd be staying home for a while."

"Not much to keep me here."

"Didn't you wear the scarf I sent with you?"

"I forgot it—left it up there. Well, don't look so startled. I can get it next time."

She turned away. "Yes, perhaps we can go past there some time. I'd like to see where you stay—and the apple orchard you tell about."

"'Tain't likely you'll get that far from home again."

He got up from the table and, fishing the key from his vest pocket, began winding his watch. As he sauntered toward the chamber door he yawned. "I'm goin' right to bed."

To Charley she explained, "Your father is awful tired tonight."

As she went about picking up the dishes, she smiled—forgot to bring the apples!

Chapter 28

It was April of '64 and spring was late coming to the prairies. Cold chilling rain brought dismal days that should have been bright and full of promise.

To Ann, confined for weeks indoors by bad weather and the dread of pneumonia, it seemed as though winter had ruthlessly pushed spring aside. The slush and snow of late March, melting slowly under cloudy skies, had turned the stage road beside the house into hub-deep mire through which settlers' wagons and the huge swaying freighters toiled tediously. The garden behind the house was a shallow pond whose muddy water rippled through a miniature submerged forest of old tattered corn stalks and leaning bean poles.

Ben, restless and worrying as usual lest spring and seedtime would never come, went daily to the farm regardless.

"I can't see what you do out there every day in this weather," Ann said fretfully.

"You just don't understand about farming on a big scale with hired help. It ain't as though we was living there—like we should be."

"Can't Jake draw a breath without you being there?" she persisted.

"There's no reason to stay here with you—sick all the time like you are. Don't seem like the bitters you're takin' are doing you much good."

"Emery came by the other day when he was in town trading. He says the Home Guards are going to start drilling again."

"First thing you know, he will be struttin' around like Sam Cook did—a big frog in a little puddle. I can't see why those men fool with being in that outfit. The Home Guards will never save the Union way out here on the prairie, and with those old-time guns! Fact is, I'm surprised the Fourth Cavalry and Sam Cook, wherever he is, haven't finished up the war before now. It's already dragged on too long."

"Emery says the copperheads down around Blue Knob have formed what they call the Knights of the Golden Circle, and they've swore to resist the draft!"

"Emery is a poor one to say anything about the draft—him with a hired substitute in the army!"

After a full minute Ben continued, "I wonder how the Home Guards would stand up in a shootin' fight with them Blue Knob Knights? They've been drillin' a lot longer than them town fellows. I hear all about it at Koepke's wagon shop. At first I figured it was just a scare story—like that one about a raid comin' up from Missouri. I suppose you've never seen one of them copperhead badges, account of you never goin' anywhere. They're just a big penny made into a button or a breast pin the women wear. After all, they've got a right to their own opinion. Could be the rebs will come out ahead. I doubt if Lincoln gets elected again. Why even Postmaster Spensley says that—and he's an employee of the 'govmunt,' as he calls it."

"Father says there will be trouble when they enforce the March draft. Here it is in the middle of April and some of the men never have reported to the provost marshal."

"I guess it will be up to old Eli Henderson to round 'em up. Nobody would want the job of going after them, down there in the brush."

"Emery says the Home Guards may be called out for regular duty. Poor Hannah is afraid to stay alone. Some of their close neighbors only three or four miles away are copperheads!"

"It would look like your brother better tend to farmin' that little place of his and let the government run down its own men. I keep wonderin' what he hears from that Buderfa boy he hired for a substitute."

"I never ask," she said coldly.

Getting early breakfast two days later, Ann saw a wet, bedraggled rider dismount at the stable and tie his horse to the fence. Not until he approached did she recognize Emery. "What are you doing in town this early on such a rainy morning?" Ann demanded as she let him into the warm kitchen.

He began pulling off his wet outer clothing and set his boots behind the stove. "I've been on guard duty all night. The copperheads threatened to burn the town and the wool warehouse if the draft is forced. Henry Laurie posted a squad on each side of town—

"How many copperheads did you arrest?" Ben asked cynically.

Emery continued calmly, as though he had not heard the question, "And all we caught was some town boys coming back from sparkin' country girls."

"I don't see how Henry or anybody else could think they'd burn the town—J. B. Goodell's wool house, wet as it is," Ben said sneeringly.

"In the Guard we have to obey orders," Emery said coldly.

"You mean even orders from a—bank clerk?"

Ann caught her brother's eye and shook her head.

After warming himself at the cookstove, Emery pulled up a chair and began eating ravenously, pausing only long enough to say, "Sister, you're as good a cook as ever."

Ben looked up in surprise.

"I stopped here because I thought Father and Mother wouldn't be up. Hannah went to stay with one of our loyal Union neighbors last night. We were afraid the Knights of the Golden Circle might do harm, knowing I'm in the Guards."

"What do you think is going to happen?" Ann asked anxiously.

"We hear that Eli Henderson and his deputy are going down to Blue Knob today. Everybody knows they're armed—maybe fifty of them."

"Eli jumped from the frying pan into the fire, didn't he?" Ben remarked quizzically.

"How was that, Ben?"

"Why, he was provost down in south part of the state—in a regular hotbed of copperheads—so he gets J. B. Goodell to fix up a transfer to a nice quiet spot up here. Eli was one of J. B.'s wheel horses in that part of the district."

Emery ate hurriedly and started home. "I've got chores to do."

Later, Ann watched Ben to see if he took the saddle horse to go to the farm. Instead, he continued across lots through the rain and entered the rear of Koepke's wagon shop.

At noon as he entered the kitchen he said excitedly, "Well, the war did come to us like I said it would. They shot Eli and the deputy—shot 'em from ambush in the timber just a little ways from your brother's place. Now the fat's in the fire!"

Ann leaned weakly against the cupboard as she said, "Oh, those poor men. Think of their families!" After a moment she asked how Ben had heard the news.

"Some settler came ridin' posthaste. He went to the post office first, not knowing who to tell first. I was in the wagon shop when Spensley came over to ask Koepke what to do. George told him to telegraph Des Moines. He did and the government is sending down another provost by stage."

"This is awful! Have you seen Emery since that happened?"

"No, but you can bet he will get called out for duty right away. They say Henry Laurie has ordered the whole Guard company to go down there as soon as the stage gets in with another provost marshal. I laugh when I think what a figure your friend Henry is going to cut — riding a horse ten miles in the rain at the head of that motley company of his, with no uniforms and not enough guns. They were begging around for horses to ride, so I had to tell them they could use mine."

Ann shook her head sadly. "I'm afraid there'll be more shooting along those brush-grown roads — and the Guards will be right in the thick of it."

"I sure hope they don't shoot my horse!"

"But Mr. Howe, what can they do with the — murderers — if they do catch them, miles from town? And we don't even have a jail."

"They are takin' wagons, too, besides the horseback riders. Likely your brother Stan will drive one of the wagons — he's so used to driving across country at night — hauling Negroes! They'll bring the dead ones in a wagon and haul prisoners in the rest. They'll have to bring in the whole fifty of 'em — they're all tarred with the same stick, as you might say."

"But what will they do with all the prisoners?"

"Maybe stack them in J. B. Goodell's wool warehouse, but they'd have to watch for fear they'd burn it down after all. When J. B. hears about it he'll likely charge the government rent," Ben said and laughed bitterly.

That evening Charley was at home only long enough to get the cow and to eat supper. As he started to put on his frock and boots, his father asked, "Where are you goin' after dark this way?"

"I'm just going over to Main Street to see if they've come from Blue Knob yet," the boy said innocently enough.

"But Mr. Howe, he is too young to be out there in that — mob. There may be shooting — or a hanging even."

"That ain't likely. Let the boy alone. He's twelve and it won't hurt him to go see what happens. Come back by nine, son, and tell us about it," Ben concluded lightly.

After the boy had gone, he continued apologetically, "They won't ketch the ones that did the shootin'—they're halfway to Missouri by this time."

An hour later, Charley dropped his boots noisily on the kitchen floor and entered the sitting room. He was more crestfallen than excited.

"You get sent home, son? What happened??"

"They must have brought in the dead men while I was home eating supper. They were layin' there on the floor of the provost's office all wrapped up in blankets. A bunch of us boys were just lookin' in the window and not hurtin' a thing, when Dave Myers came along. He was walkin' up and down in front, with a shotgun on his shoulder and he says, 'Beat it, you kids—and don't come back.' Made me kinda sick—him a clerk in Harve Blue's store struttin' around and giving orders!"

"But you didn't come right home, now did you?"

"No, sir, we sneaked down across the track to the wool warehouse to see 'em unload prisoners. There were two wagonsful come in. Gee! it was exciting."

"Did you see your uncle Emery anywhere?" Ann asked anxiously.

"Oh, yes, Aunt Ann, he was drivin' the second wagon, and he had the one they said was the captain of the copperheads. And was he mad—I mean the copperhead. He says—"

"Don't repeat it before—her. You can tell me later."

"I was just going to tell you the way he was complainin'. He was sure he was going to ketch pneumonia or consumption from riding all the way to town in that open wagon. Finally I heard uncle Emery tell him to shut up—and that if he'd have pulled his coat around himself he'd not be so cold and wet!"

"Did you see anything of my horse, son?"

"No, sir."

"How many prisoners did they bring in?" Ben asked, half-wishing he had gone down to see the excitement.

"They brought in two loads—five or six to the wagon, besides the driver and a guard with a gun. Guess who was Guard on Emery's wagon? Henry Laurie!"

158

"I told you he'd not ride a horse, didn't I now?" Ben said triumphantly, turning to Ann.

"Some of the prisoners were awful mad," Charley continued, "and some were scared. We heard one fellow beggin' to go home so he could milk his cows. He says, 'My woman cain't milk a drop and them bags will spoil before tomorrow.' Then Mr. Laurie spoke up real sharp, 'You ain't goin' home tomorrow or the next day either. You are goin' to be held for hearing before a Justice of the Peace, for murder'. Then the fellow says—"

"Don't repeat it!"

Charley continued excitedly, "And another fellow said his wife was all alone down there in the timber and she was goin' to have a baby most—"

"Don't say any more about it," Ben said sternly. "You say you didn't see anything of my horse?"

"No, sir."

"I suppose the Guards sent you home after that?"

"We got too close trying to see and hear it all. Gee, it was fun!"

"It's nine o'clock and time we were all in bed," Ben declared, getting up stiffly and going to the kitchen for a drink. "You coming, Ann?"

Aware of every strange sound outside, Ann lay for hours beside the impassive Ben, who was undisturbed by her violent spells of coughing. All her worries and fears came crowding in upon her consciousness. After the clock struck twelve, she slipped from bed and went to see if Alice was covered. Returning through the sitting room, she brushed against the mound of quilt pieces on the table and paused to finger them thoughtfully. Perhaps tomorrow I can do more on them, she thought.

At the kitchen window she peered across lots to Main Street. One lone light, a lantern set on the boardwalk, cast giant animated shadows on the high false front of the provost's office as a lone guard paced back and forth disconsolately in the cold drizzle that had begun again.

Reluctant to return to bed, she continued watching the pacing figure. Mr. Henderson is dead—in there on the floor—it caught up with him today—the *thing* I've fought off these two years past. For him it is all over—how strange to envy a man I never saw but twice. Somebody will take up where he left off—but I have so much to do—bringing up Alice.

At dawn, as she raised herself wearily from bed, a bright red splotch stained her pillow. Quickly she turned it away lest Mr. Howe would see it.

Stephen Barrett pushed open the kitchen door and came in with his arm load of wood, and dropped it noisily into the box beside the cookstove. Then he straightened up and, brushing the litter of the wood from his shirt, turned to look inquisitively at Doshia, who stood silent at the window, looking out across the slough that separated the townsite from the college, whose plain boxlike new brick buildings on the hill were catching the level rays of the June sunset. She had not answered his cheery greeting. A glance told him something was wrong; her shoulders, stooped worse than usual, spelled dejection or sorrow, perhaps both.

He crossed the room to put an arm around her shoulder, and with a hand gently raised her bowed head, as if to read in her moist eyes the worries that confounded her. "You don't need to tell me you are worried and upset over something; I know you are. Has our youngest son's sharp spoken wife been nagging again?" Then his voice dropped and he spoke gently, "Then it is Ann; you've been to see her today?"

Yes," she nodded, "and it wasn't good, what I saw there today."

"Tell me, my dear; it isn't so bad if we face it together."

"It isn't anything new," Doshia said in a hushed tone. "We've known ever since Ben moved her to town over a year ago that she was bad off."

"But why did things with her seem worse today, my dear? Was she in bed again?" Stephen persisted.

"No, she was up, and hobbling about. It was a lot of things all put together that made me realize"—she hesitated before finishing the sentence— "her time is short."

"How did she seem to be worse today?"

"It is in her face, Stephen, that pitiful, haunted look in her tired eyes, with her face so guant and hollow cheeked, an unnatural flush and her lips so colorless."

"But mother, that is nothing new; she has looked pretty peeked for two years now, ever since the spotted fever. She has kept going though she wasn't able. I know she feels she must, to keep Ben satisfied. What else discouraged you so badly? Did she say something to hurt you?"

"No, Stephen, it was what I saw. She tried to hide it, but I saw the stain. She is coughing up blood. You know that is a bad sign; Belle Walsh was that way before she died of consumption; remember?

"Yes, that does look bad," Stephen said sadly, "and there isn't anything the doctors can do; they say there is no cure."

"We can't just let her die! If we keep praying and praying, and taking care of her, don't you think God will spare her for us and for Alice?"

"We will do everything we can. I will hire a girl to do her housework, if Ben will allow her to stay. That would help Ann get more rest."

All through the summer, Ann kept up the pretense of keeping house, with a succession of kitchen help, black and white; none, though, seemed to satisfy Ben's incessant, exacting demand for "something fit to eat."

Through those months, Ann alternated between being in bed or listlessly working around the house, yet steadily growing weaker.

It was mid-September when she took to her bed, there in the little chamber on the side next to the street. Young Dr. Harrison said: "You keep trying to do more than you should, as long as you are up and around. Let this hired girl do the work; you be the queen."

Ben, returning from the farm, seemed surprised to find Ann in bed with Doshia and Philo watching over her. "I knew she wasn't feeling very well this morning, but I thought she was just a little upset, likely something she ate."

Young Harrison sent word to Ben he wanted to see him, next day, and when Ben reluctantly stayed home from the farm to meet him, he was told Ann could not live long.

Ben seemed surprised and almost shocked. "Why, she was up and did quite a baking just the other day!"

Doc Harrison was firm, as he continued, "I want her moved over to Barretts right away. It will be easier for her mother to take care of her there. She must not be left alone again."

"But Doc, this is her home; she won't be content over there."

Comfortably settled in the downstairs bedroom that had once been hers, Ann did find some slight, belated comfort, with Doshia waiting on her hand and foot.

Philo was back and forth several times a day, often bringing odd bits of news from John; much more encouraging now that Atlanta had fallen. She retold some of John's lighter adventures, and she brought some relief to a tense household during the long hours she sat at Ann's bedside.

Once, Ann murmured weakly, "It won't be long till he will be coming home to see you, and Alice will fall in love with him all over again." But she gave no hint that she, herself, ever expected to see him.

Later, Ben came to Stephen's twice a day to ask about Ann, though he seldom stayed long; his visits cut short by his apologetic, "I must be going now, but I'll try to get back later." He seemed to sense the unspoken, yet bitter, resentment, amounting almost to hatred, that Stephen and Doshia felt toward him.

Nothing Ben could ever do or say would offset for them the grief and resentment his selfish indifference had caused.

They waited bitterly for the inevitable end.

Cheerful words and difficult smiles could not deceive the sick woman. She knew her life was ebbing away, and, with the apathy of the very sick, she faced it calmly.

Then it was the last week in October, and things looked worse.

Had she kept up her dairy for that day, those yellow, faded pages might well have read, "Oct. 25 Am so weak, Mr. Howe came to Father's to see me. Said he is not going to the farm tomorrow."

In that chill, quiet hour just before dawn, Ann slipped away to face the Great Beyond; completing in thirty-six years the circle of existence, to be well born, to live courageously, and to die with a faith that knows no end.

They buried her, at Stephen's insistence, on that quiet hilltop in the new cemetery, in the afternoon of a short fall day. And even as the mound was smoothed flat, the dry wind-blown autumn leaves mingled with the fall garden flowers that covered the bare mound.

Slowly the now sorrowing husband and the little girl with her grieving grandparents were driven down the hill, across the slough, back to the lonely white house on Broad Street.

And once more the bare little cemetery was still. Overhead, outlined against a clear blue sky, a wavering vee of wild fowl winged their way homeward, guided by a faith that likewise never questions.

More than a century has passed since that chill October day when Ann was laid to rest. The cemetery is no longer a bare, unkept acreage, sparsely occupied. Rather, it is a place of well-ordered beauty and bears the name Hazelwood, for the wild shrubs that once covered its slopes. Now it is the resting place of thousands of others, who once called Goodell home. The spindly elms and maples have grown to spreading giants that cast a pleasant shade over the resting place of the colony folks gathered there in the "old part." The coarse prairie grass and the hazel brush have long since gone, and green clipped lawns and flowering shrubs cover those hilltops.

There beside the road that winds gently along the hill stands the simple headstone with the faded inscription

ANN BARRETT

Wife of B. Howe

1828   1864

Postlude

The town of Goodell, Powhatan County, is not found on a modern Iowa map. Yet there is such a place if one can identify it. Travelers on a transcontinental highway pass through its quiet tree-shaded streets unmindful of its past. They admire its streets arched over by noble elms, not knowing this was once a treeless prairie ridge.

The highway of today follows across town the northern boundary of the old townsite. Approaching from the east, the traveler passes a not-too-new grade school they named for Colonel Cook, who drilled anxious recruits in the park, the spring of '61. The street curves carefully around the tree shaded campus of Goodell University to avoid bespoiling its trees and shaded walks. Beyond the campus a short way a boulder marks the site of the long cabin of 1854. Farther westward the highway passes the site of Homer Hamill's square, boxlike farmhouse. Nearby they built a grade school and honored that early teacher Len Packard by naming it for him while he was still alive. Beyond the small brick school the highway is the same route Ben Howe drove his creaking ox drawn cart that Sabbath in the fall of '55 when he took Laura to J.B. Goodell's house to die.

Modern day engineers decreed the highway should veer off a bit to follow the old stage road. So the cabin on the ridge does not stand on the main road. And from the height of the ridge one looks across the valley to the "state road." There, where the covered wagons passed, swift autos and trucks whisk their passengers and freight. The stage driver's horn has long since been silenced. From the cabin site instead, one hears the diesels of modern trains on what they once called the M & M Railroad, as they glide down the valley through the "timber 40" Stephen owned—following the survey line Granville Dodge staked in '52.

Ann lies buried there on the hilltop in Hazelwood within sight of the old farm where she lived those few short years. Beside her lies also the lonely Laura, with her newborn babe. And close beside is the firm and kindly Cordelia, who followed Ben to distant California in '82. Ben does not rest there on that hilltop beside those three whom in turn he held dear. Instead, a granite marker bears his name and the simple phrase "Pioneer of 1854." The wayward Charley lies beside the Laura who bore him and the Ann who tried so hard to win him with love. Over them all tower the century-old trees, some that Emery planted when the cemetery was new and half-covered with hazel brush.

Nearby is the tall spirelike granite monument with "Barrett" in faded lettering. Stephen and his beloved Doshia are there—Emery the dependable and his Hannah the vivacious. In one corner of the lot stands a bronze marker bearing a small weather beaten flag. It calls attention that here lies John Peck who went out to save the Union in '61. Beside him lies his devoted Philo who bravely saw him off to war and waited patiently for his return to live out their all-too-short life together.

Yes, they are all there in the older section of the cemetery—those whose names have filled these pages—the pioneers—the first families. They and two generations who followed them are fast being gathered there. Some found fame, others fortune, but the many received only the plaudits due honest upright lives.

On the crest of the far hill in the southeast corner, Amos Longley rests beneath a simple marker, his life span closed that spring of '65, just as the neighbor boys were returning from Appomatox and Atlanta. And Lyman, the son Cordelia bore him lies nearby, alongside his beloved Alice, whom Stephen and Doshia raised to womanhood after Ann's death in '64.

There you have the story—Ann's story—Goodell as it was and as one would see it now. The church, the college, and the quiet pleasant little town—all these are the enduring monument to the people who braved the dangers and inconveniences of the raw prairie to establish them. To us who come after, these people were not heroes or heroines, but flesh-and-blood humans with the frailties and faults of mankind.

It is the hope of the author that *Cabin on the Second Ridge* will help just a bit to keep fresh in modern-day minds the story of the settling of the Middle West. Thus history is made to seem real by dealing in terms of real people who had their part, however small, in that westward movement.

I might add right here—that "Ann" was my own grandmother and this book was created from her authentic diary that she carefully kept—until several days before her death.